Penguin Book 2735
Cobbler's Dream

The great-granddaughter of Charles Dickens,
Monica Dickens was educated at St Paul's Girls'
School. She has been writing novels and
autobiographical books since she was twenty-two,
when she wrote *One Pair of Hands* about her
experiences as a cook-general, the only job that her
upbringing as a débutante had fitted her for.

During the war, Miss Dickens worked as a nurse
in a hospital and subsequently took a job in a
munitions factory, turning out Spitfires. During the
latter part of the war she was again working in a
hospital. 'I would like to make it clear,' she says,
'that I did not take these jobs in order to write
books. The books just came out of the experiences.'

After the war Miss Dickens gave up nursing to
concentrate on her writing, and has published several
novels, of which the latest is *The Room Upstairs*.
She is married to Commander Roy Stratton of the
U.S. Navy, and has two daughters.

Monica Dickens

Cobbler's Dream

Penguin Books

Penguin Books Ltd, Harmondsworth,
Middlesex, England
Penguin Books Australia Ltd, Ringwood,
Victoria, Australia

First published by Michael Joseph 1963
Published in Penguin Books 1967
Copyright © Monica Dickens, 1963

Made and printed in Great Britain by
Hazell Watson & Viney Ltd, Aylesbury, Bucks
Set in Linotype Times

This book is sold subject to the condition that
it shall not, by way of trade or otherwise, be lent,
re-sold, hired out, or otherwise circulated without
the publisher's prior consent in any form of
binding or cover other than that in which it is
published and without a similar condition
including this condition being imposed on the
subsequent purchaser

To Bobby

Chapter One

Black and bristling, the long patch of brushwood waited in the blossoming hedge, firm as a new toothbrush.

At either side, the small white flags moved gently against a colourless sky, and a lark went up, hovering his song.

The song disappeared in a surge of hoofs up the turf of the hill, and in a moment they were pouring over the jump like water, like waves rising to break, in a thunder of flung mud and curses. Then they were gone, bunched together for the downhill turn and fanning out over the low bank on to the sticky plough.

A man with a black mud face climbed somehow back on to his wild-eyed circling horse, and galloped hopelessly after them. Behind him, the trim line of the new brushwood fence was torn and broken. A ragged bunch of twigs leaned out like a falling tooth.

A man in a raincoat and a long-legged girl in red woollen stockings climbed through a gap in the hedge from the other side, and the boy who was holding the reins of the grey horse struggling on the ground shouted at them to get a vet.

Off to the left, beyond a white rail fence, most of the old horses had not even looked up as the surge and thunder of the race broke over the hilltop jump. The thin thoroughbred mare with the scarred chest had trotted the stiff stilts of her legs to the fence to gaze, head-up, long ears stretched, until the last hoofs had squelched away downhill. Then she dropped her head mildly to graze again, her ancient teeth pulling the grass bluntly up by the roots, so that she could only press out the sweetness and let the tuft of turf fall.

None of the horses raised their heads when the shot cracked the damp air, and by the last race of the day, when the rain was beginning, even the old racehorse did not look up as the dark wet horses crashed through what was left of the brushwood fence.

The point-to-point crowd were going home, wheels spinning in the creamed mud, jeeps bucketing past triumphant, boots slogging through the ruined car park, when Dora came to the gate of the top field and whistled. In the distance, round the side of the hill, she could see the crawl of cars, congealing each time someone stuck in the gateway, and the last damp enthusiasts drifting back across the course.

It was the last meeting of the season. Tomorrow the tents and ropes and flags would be taken down, the chestnut paling rolled. The cows would be put back on the sour trodden grass where the crowds had milled and cast down betting tickets, and the farmer would harrow the patch of plough.

'Who won the last race?' Dora asked the spotted pony who was first into the fenced lane that led to the stable yard. The top of his rump was square, and his back flat as a table from years of spangled ladies dancing on him and making pyramids. The pony checked her briefly for sugar and walked on, followed by the yellow Mongolian horse with a cow's high angular hips, and the faded black pit pony who sagged in the middle like a sprung sofa.

Ronnie Stryker, lounging at the yard gate in skin tight jeans and cowboy boots, a match in his mouth for want of a cigarette, let them through one by one to walk across the cobbles to their own boxes. The horses who were already in banged on their doors and swung their heads about and made false ferocious faces of greed.

Slugger Jones and Uncle were taking round the feeds: Slugger concealed under a trenchcoat to his ankles, and the Captain's old fishing hat turned down all round with a fly still in it, Uncle a goblin with a mealy sack across his bent shoulders.

'The last woman who saw you in that sack said she felt sorrier for you than for the horses,' the Captain told him.

'So she should be.' Uncle leered under his witch's nose. 'No one here now anyway.'

'Someone's coming in.'

Dozens of people went along the road past the farm every

8

day, and some of them threw a remark, flippant, or soppy, or cynical, at the notice board arched over the gate, and a few of them stopped to see what was inside.

The Captain always let them in. Not for what they would put in the collection box. The year's harvest from the red and white box would not pay the water bill. It was for pride in his horses. And one day Roxanne would come. One day she would be on that road, going somewhere, coming from somewhere, and she would stop. She would have to stop, because the sign said Horses.

'We saw the sign,' the girl in the red stockings told Dora, 'and I said to my friend: "How sweet," and made him stop. Home of Rest for Horses. "How sweet," I said.'

'Yes, it is sweet,' said Dora shortly. She was suspicious of girls who were tall and supple and looked good in the rain. She was busy, but the Captain was mixing a poultice in the saddle room that had no saddles, so she went with them along the boxes that lined three sides of the yard.

She showed them the gipsy's horse, with a hole where her eye used to be. She showed them the donkeys and the Shetlands and the roan horse from Ireland which had once lifted off a woman's church hat and eaten it. She showed them the brewery horse with the behind like a beer barrel, and she showed them the dusty brown mare who had been on her way to Buckingham Palace and never got there.

'A man was riding her from Cumberland to London with a petition for the Queen about common grazing rights,' she told them. 'But old Puss broke down a few miles from here, and the man went on by bus.'

Most people asked why he had never come back for the horse, but the girl's mind did not work that way. She said, 'I prefer the trains myself,' and went on to the next loose box.

She looked over all the doors, clucking and chirping, but most of the horses had their tails turned and their heads in the manger. Spot came to lick her hand, and she fancied herself special. 'He likes me! They know, you see. They know when you –' She jerked her hand away as the old circus pony tried the edge of his teeth thoughtfully on the palm.

The man who was with her put his hands quickly into his

raincoat pockets, but Dora said at the next door: 'Don't worry about Nigger. You couldn't get near his mouth.' She told them how he had come to them, a farmer's horse stolen out of a field, ridden all night by a gang of boys with a piece of wire in his mouth for a bridle, and left torn and bleeding in a gravel pit with half his tongue gone.

The girl looked sick, and the man licked his lips, as if he could feel the wire, and said nervously: 'Shouldn't he have been put away then?'

'He would have been,' Dora said, 'but we got to him first.'

'At the races,' the girl said, 'there was a horse fell and broke its leg, right at the fence where we were, and they shot it. Wasn't that terrible? I wish I'd known about this place. They could have brought it here.'

'Not with a broken leg,' Dora said. 'Horses are too heavy. They can't mend.'

'I thought it was terrible.' The girl did not always register information. 'We were right there, you know. Right there, as close as I am to you. "How cruel," I kept saying. "The poor beautiful beast," and the man who had been riding it said: "Shut up. It's bad enough without that." He had one of those ever-so voices. You know. They don't care. Then when he took off his fancy red cap and wiped the mud off his face, I saw that he was only a very young boy really. And then, you know,' said the girl, with a faraway look in her eyes because it was an idea, 'I thought perhaps that he did care.'

'If we go now,' the man said, 'we might make the Antelope for dinner.'

When it was dark, the old horses ruminated on hay, or stood thinking of nothing, like chickens, or dropped into the light, nervous sleep of an animal whose chief weapon is speed to escape. The pit pony was lying down, forelegs tucked under him, eyes closed, nose resting lightly in the straw. The Weaver, who had once carried Royalty on parade, rocked gently from foot to foot, swinging his gaunt bay head back and forth over his door. The two Shetland ponies stood head to tail, although there were no flies, and one of the donkeys lay flat out with his head under the manger, as if he were dead.

In other stables, the horses that had raced that day rested in bandages and expensive initialed rugs, the rain and sweat and mud groomed off them, the burrs and twigs brushed out of their splendid tails. The one that would not race again was a mound at the back of the slaughterer's shed. Under the stained tarpaulin, a hoof stuck out, packed with a clod of turf from the hill.

Chapter Two

Half an hour after she had ridden into the yard, shouting for Paul, the child went back into the stable and beat the pony.

When Paul looked over the door, she was standing with the whip in her fist, breathing hard. The pony was rammed against the far wall with his head up, rolling his eye at her and shivering.

'Why,' Paul said, not making it a question, because Chrissy had done this sort of thing before.

She turned and gave him the special stare she reserved for employees and girls who went to school by bus, as if she were slapping them up and down with a paintbrush dipped in mud. There was no guilt on her face at being caught. She was twelve, coarse-featured, with dry hairdresser's curls on the ends of her colourless hair, thighs too fat for riding and pale stubby hands, like cheeses.

'I told you. He bucked after the jump. Twice.' She came to the door and opened it, pushing against Paul's chest.

'I told you not to use the spurs. Why beat him now? He can't remember.' Paul went into the pony. Cobby stayed by the wall, leaning against it with his legs braced. Sweat was breaking out on him in streaks, like blood springing under a lash. The boy said his name, and he swung round his head to look at him, his ears moving back and forth suspiciously.

'He'll remember all right.' The pony jerked his head up again, as Chrissy smacked her whip against the outside of the door.

'He'll remember pain.' Paul stood back from the pony. He would move to touch him later, when the child was gone.

'I've told my father all along,' she said in that high Chrissy voice, thick and nasal because her mother would not risk having her adenoids out, 'He'll have to get me something better. This beastly thing is useless. He makes a mistake every time.'

'It's you who's useless,' Paul said, because there were times when he did not care if the child got him fired or not, and he would not have stayed this long if it had not been for the Cobbler. 'He didn't make a mistake the year before last, when he was properly ridden.'

Chrissy could not deny it, for that was why her father had bought the chestnut pony, so she stuck out her underlip and said: 'That Mason girl. She shouldn't be in juvenile jumping anyway. Everyone knows she's been sixteen for years.'

And then she remembered, and her sulky face lifted into a mean rodent smile. 'Anyway, you don't know what happened the year before last. You were in gaol.' She triumphed off across the yard in her shiny boots, swatting her whip at harmless things like drainpipes and buckets, looking for insects to stamp on.

It was true. Paul had been, if not actually in gaol, in the Borstal institution proper to his age.

It had not technically been his fault, but he had given up saying 'It wasn't my fault' to people who were sick of hearing juvenile delinquents unload responsibility on to parents, schools, psychiatrists, the Government – anyone behind whom they could shuffle with a chance of getting away with it.

It had been his fault too – the actual crime. He had gone into it willingly, even with relish. But the degree of the blame which fell on him was not, and it would have been only probation, not Borstal, if the Hyena and his lot had not let him down.

Why had he kept his mouth shut and let them get away with it? The Hyena . . . more like a lizard with that greenish-black hair slick on the narrow sloping head. But the laugh, the cackle. It curdled you. Borstal was safe, at least, and if Paul had been at large and the Hyena inside, he would have heard that laugh in his dreams until the day when he heard it just behind him in a dark alley, and knew that the Hyena was out and seeking revenge.

When Paul was free, he had gone once more to his mother. This time the door was not locked against him, but she was not there. A strange family was in the house, and no one knew where she had gone, or if they did, they were not telling, not with Paul a disgrace to the street, and the Borstal officer standing there beside him, trying unsuccessfully to look like everybody's uncle.

Chrissy's father was on the Youth Committee because 'one had to pull one's weight' in a town on whose crowded park benches he had slept thirty years ago rawboned and hungry in the shadow of the idle factories. He had offered to take Paul into his stables, since 'the boy seems to be interested in horses – one point in his favour, Mr Chairman, you'll agree.' It was a satisfactory proposal. He got all the credit for a gesture more generous and practical than his colleagues' anxious theories, but his groom would have the trouble of training Paul, and seeing that he did not run away or steal.

Paul instantly disliked the groom, who wore his cap dead flat like a kettle lid and treated the horses as if they were no more than horses. He was afraid of Chrissy's father, who had left poverty and failure too far behind to remember, like being born. He was discouraged by the mother's instability, in some ways worse than his own mother's predictable neglect, and he had always hated Chrissy since long ago when he had seen her at a local show, a brat of eight in a precocious bowler hat, riding a pony that was too good for her in spurs. But when they bought the chestnut pony, he knew that he would stay.

Cobby was golden in full sun and copper in the evening light, with quarters round like an orange, a square chest and a neck like a stallion. He was styled like a small horse, but his head was pure pony, square-nosed, with short curved ears and a jaunty dark blue eye. His full name was Cobbler's Dream. He had begun to make his mark as a show jumper, and could have gone on to glory, but not with Chrissy. She was the kind of child a horse hates, and in their first show together, she had pulled him so cruelly off balance that Paul had to go behind the stewards' tent because he could not watch.

The day after he caught Chrissy beating the Cobbler, Paul rode him out to exercise while she was at school. When he shied at a piece of paper and then again at nothing, it could have been nervousness from yesterday, but when he stumbled twice on a smooth piece of turf, there was something wrong. He never stumbled. He had small, close-packed hoofs like little drums, each one thudding neatly down as if that particular piece of ground had existed since time began for nothing else than to receive his stride.

Two days later, Chrissy had him out in the jumping ring, for the first show of the season was only a week away. She was iron-fisted as ever, with her jockey cap rammed down over her eyes and her sullen underlip lying on her face like a caterpillar. When she finally let him go at the brush, he cleared it awkwardly, nothing like his usual rubber-ball style.

'Give him a chance!' Paul shouted, and she turned to make a face at him, but at the next jump, it was clearly Cobby who did not give the child a chance. The groom had called to her to keep her hands forward, and she did, but the pony came into it all wrong, hit the jump with his square red chest and fell in a tangle of legs and rails and fat child looping a slow loop on to the wet grass.

She was not hurt. She had good shock absorbers where she landed, but her howls raised windows in the house a hundred yards away. The groom had to take her back to the house, to show that he thought more of her than the horse, for his wife liked the cottage that went with the job. The pony seemed all right, so on the way back to the stable Paul hopped him over a small log that he had jumped a hundred times without checking his stride.

Then he knew. In the stable, he suddenly flung up his hand at the side of the pony's head. The fear was reality.

When the vet came, he told Chrissy's father what Paul already knew. Cobbler's Dream was totally blind in the left eye.

After some tests, he said that it appeared to be an injury to the optic nerve, caused by some kind of blow. 'The pony has knocked his head when he was turned out perhaps, sir?'

The vet was a perfectionist in a town where money often spoke louder than finesse, but there were five classy horses here and a lot of expensive fuss about injections and blood tests, so the soap was lathered.

'He's never turned out,' Chrissy's father said impatiently. 'Too risky. If I told you what I paid for him.'

Soap was one thing, but the vet did not have to be impressed into begging him to tell. 'Then he must have done it in the stable, sir,' he said. 'It's just bad luck. He could have hit his head almost anywhere else and done no harm.'

'Bad luck!' Chrissy's father rounded on Paul, nervously chewing hay in the yard outside the box full of élite, which included the mother in a poodle jacket and shoes like arrowheads, and the groom, who could not be found to blame, because his last employer had a title. 'Did you do this, boy? A clever pony doesn't bang himself about. He's been hit, that's clear. If you did this, Paul, by God, I – I'll have you sent back where you came from!'

'He's probably too old,' Chrissy said calmly. 'He's almost eighteen.' Her father had not told her that Paul had been in Borstal, but with her genius for hurting, she had found out, and so there were very few people in that neighbourhood who did not know.

'Did you do this?' The man's broad face was crimson, the nose mottling to purple. 'Not that he'd tell,' he said to the embarrassed vet. 'The boy's a chronic liar.'

Paul shook his head. Even these people knew how he felt about the Cobbler, even if they did not understand. The suggestion was too absurd to answer, and whatever he said, it would be called a lie. Chrissy would not look at him. He stared hard at her, trying to force her to look, but she would not turn her head. She was leaning against the manger and biting her nails; not stroking the pony, as another child would do with an injured pet. He was not her pet. He was just a vehicle on which she had planned to win fame.

But now no more. Cobby would always be blind in that eye, the vet said, and he would be lucky if the other eye did not eventually go too. Chrissy's father, who believed that anything would come right if you only paid enough, brought an impressive gentleman in a brown suit and bowler to match down from the Royal Veterinary College in London, but the verdict was the same.

As a show jumper, Cobbler's Dream was useless, finished, and Chrissy's father was going to have him destroyed and collect the insurance.

When Paul heard that, he went into his small room behind the tack room, where the pin-up pictures were horses, not girls.

He lay face down on the low iron bed, not crying, but tensed tight, clutching the edge of the mattress, fighting the terrible feeling in his head and limbs that he would go berserk and scream and yell and hurt somebody. Take a gun and shoot somebody.

When he was younger, he sometimes used to scream and throw the furniture about, and when his mother was drunk, she would throw it back and scream too, for it was she who had taught him the hysteria of noise. He had done it once or twice when he first went to Borstal, to call attention to himself among the regimented pack. Unimpressed, they had told him to grow up, and left him no alternative.

At fourteen, it had been easy to go berserk. At eighteen, it might turn out to be a creaking affair, like an old man playing hopscotch. It would not help the Cobbler if he made a fool of himself.

When he had grown calmer, he got up and went to the house. He tried to reason with Chrissy's father. He pleaded, suggested work that Cobby could still do, good homes that he could go to.

'Whose pony is it?' was all the man would say. Except when he said: 'Considering that I'm still not sure it wasn't your fault, you'd better shut up and remember who's been kind to you.'

Outside, Paul turned and looked back at the lighted window where the man sat reading the evening paper, his ugly blunt fingers round a glass. Kind! Don't make me laugh. You can't take life away from that pony just because he's no use to you. Who made you God all of a sudden? If you kill the Cobbler, Paul said to him in silence, no hell is bad enough for you.

In the year that he had been here, his ramshackle life had grown round the chestnut pony like a man in love. He had known horses, many of them on his grandfather's farm, where he had spent the intervals of his childhood in between his mother's bouts of love or guilt or loneliness, when she dragged him back to town with her. Later, the brewery horses had been like long-lost friends to him, shining, moustached, cared for with greater pride than the beer. He had felt close to a horse often, but never, as sometimes with Cobby, as if he actually was that horse: feeling the high back teeth inside his own head when the pony was grinding his grain, knowing on his own skin how it felt when he shivered off a fly.

He responded to Paul's thought, as a dog trotting ahead will stop and look round if you concentrate on him. The pony would always turn his head, or lift it from the gleanings of his hay to look up and over the door at the boy's unspoken call.

Long ago, Paul's grandmother used to tell him stories of animals she had talked to, and what they had said. He had believed her then, and the belief had returned, with Cobbler's Dream.

How to explain this to anyone? Least of all to Chrissy's parents, who had only taken up horses in the first place because it was a more expensive hobby than golf.

Chrissy had avoided Paul, not surprisingly. It was not until the end of three terrible days, most of which he spent with Cobby when he was not pleading or arguing with his owners, that he managed to catch her alone. Her parents were out, and when the chauffeur brought her home from school, Paul was waiting for her behind the big yew by the front door.

When the car drove off, he stepped out and said in his roughest gangland voice: 'I want to talk to you.'

Chrissy squeaked, but he pulled her round the corner of the house and into the back hall where they kept the boots and fishing rods.

'Let me go!' The fat child opened her mouth to scream, but Paul put his hand over it and only took it away when she bit him.

'You hit Cobby on the head,' he said quickly, to keep her quiet. She looked at him shiftily for a second to see how much he knew. Then she stuck her frizzed head in the air and said: 'You taste disgusting, Borstal boy,' and moved her lips and tongue in and out as if she had eaten a bad shrimp.

'You blinded him,' Paul said.

'If you think so, why don't you tell them?' Although they hated each other at this moment perhaps more than ever, she put herself on his side against her parents by calling them Them, and Paul knew that she was afraid.

'They wouldn't believe me. You have to tell them,' Paul said.

'You can't stand back and let them kill your pony because of what you did.'

'He should be put out of his misery.' She was turning to go, but Paul caught her roughly by the wrist with the charm bracelet.

'He's not in misery. He can't jump, but he could hack around. The vet said so.'

Chrissy tried to pull her hand away, and when she could not, she shrugged and let it go limp. 'And stumble and kill someone. No thanks. He's going tomorrow by the way.' She watched Paul closely with her pebble eyes. 'Daddy has found a grey that was second in the Pony Club finals last year, and it's coming on trial. Didn't they tell you?'

It was like a stopper being taken out, and all the sap of life being drained away. 'What time is the vet coming?' Paul managed to ask.

'Not the vet, you dope. The knacker. You get more money if he's taken away alive. Daddy told me. About twelve pounds for a carcass. Thirty or forty if they kill it at their own place, because they can sell it for human consumption. To eat, you know,' she added, enunciating the words as if he were deaf. 'You'd be surprised how many people in the Midlands like horse meat.'

Her teeth had wires on them because Nature had stuck them out like the rat she was. They were almost knocked in then, and the wires superfluous, but Paul slackened his fingers, and she looked at her wrist for a moment critically, shaking the ugly bracelet, and then went into the house.

When Paul announced that he was leaving, the mother said thank you, that would save her embarrassment, since Chrissy had told them how roughly he had treated her, and they had been going to send for him to say that he must go. His probation had expired several weeks ago. They need no longer be responsible for him. He should be ashamed of himself for terrifying a helpless child and proving himself so ungrateful for all that had been done for him, etcetera, etcetera. She was in a lecturing mood and hard to stop.

Where would he go? He had no idea, but he knew what he was going to do. He went to Chrissy's father and offered him forty pounds for the Cobbler, the knacker's highest price. The broad red man laughed. He was busy checking accounts, but he took time to raise his head and laugh.

Paul went to Chrissy. 'This is blackmail,' he said out of the side of his mouth. 'Either I tell them what you did, or you go and beg your father to let me buy Cobby, using all the phoney charm.' He did not think she had any charm, phoney or not, but her father did.

She was as mean as twenty grown-ups, but she was still a child. Paul put his hands on her neck and made a horror film face at her, and she was afraid, and did what he asked, although it was possible that her father might not even have minded the truth of what she had done. They were that kind of people.

Paul waited until all the lights were out in the ugly pebbled house and in the cottage where the groom slept neat and short-legged beside his contented wife, before he came out through the tack room carrying his shoes, because the yard was gravelled.

He did not speak or whistle in the stable yard, but two of the horses called to him, in the futile hope that it was breakfast.

'Shut up,' he said at the door of the box, as Cobby dropped the trumpet of his head and fluttered his nose in a softer greeting. 'You want to spoil everything?' He had cut up some feed bags earlier, and he tied the sacking round the pony's feet with baling string and led him out of the stable. Not stealing. He had included the price of the halter in the money he had posted to Chrissy's father that afternoon, all his savings except twenty-eight shillings. It was too risky to hand it over personally, in case he laughed and said that he had changed his mind. That was why Paul was getting out now. Too risky to wait until morning.

The pony stumbled a lot, mostly because of the mufflers, for he was adjusting himself to being one-eyed, but Paul did not take off the sacking until they were past the last houses and out into the country. There was no moon, but the sky was full of lightless radiance that kept away the dark. A thin vapour of mist floated just above the grass, and the trees rose rootless out of the shrouded hedges.

Paul walked fast, and Cobby paced his neatly sprung legs

beside him, swinging his head round to peer at things which he could sense, but could not see. It felt like an adventure, a thousand times more exciting than that shivering wait on the river steps by the warehouse. It felt like a desperate rescue, although the pony was his, because the morning might have brought Chrissy's father going back on his word. It might have brought the knacker.

As the miles went by, it grew darker and colder, and the road grew harder and the hills steeper, but it was the night of all nights, because he had something of his own. He was alone with the Cobbler and the world was theirs.

Chapter Three

His hair curled like a wet black retriever, and there was about him a look of enduring boyhood which would be particularly irritating to someone like Ronnie Stryker, who had been jaded before his teens.

Ronnie called him Curly, and stuck to it. Dora never called him anything but Paul. She had fought against being Dossie at home ever since she was old enough to feel the humiliation of a forced nickname. Uncle called him Laddie, and Slugger Jones called him nothing, since he never addressed anyone directly, but only through himself. When the Captain first saw him, he had called him a thief, or at least asked him if he was one.

Dora had been alone in the yard when Paul and the pony came weaving in. They had walked all night, and when they stopped under the arched entrance, Paul leaned against the wall because he could not stand up any longer.

Dora was coming out of the feed shed with a tub of mash for the old pit pony with the useless teeth. 'Customer?' she asked, looking at Cobby, who was sagging, with his neck stuck out like a decrepit cab horse.

When Paul told her where they were from, she said: 'If he can walk that far, he shouldn't be in here,' and wished that she had not, for the boy said hoarsely: 'You've got to take him.'

When Dora fetched the Captain from the house, Paul had told him that the pony was a family pet who had been blinded in an accident. His people could not afford to keep a horse that could not work. They would have him destroyed unless the Farm would take him.

The Captain listened sympathetically. Many of the horses in his stable had been under the death sentence before they found reprieve here. But when he saw the Cobbler, dragging hay out of the rack in the corner box as if he had not eaten for weeks, he said at once: 'I know that pony. Seen it jump at shows.'

'You can't have,' said Dora, who took people at their declared value and had recently got them all into trouble by accepting a horse that a woman had stolen out of a field because it had a sad face. 'It's been pulling his father's junk cart.'

'Junk my foot,' the Captain said, beetling at Paul with his jaw and eyebrows set in what he believed was a look of craggy militarism. 'This pony has never pulled anything in its life but hay. I saw him win at the Three Counties. Year before last. The Mason girl. She outgrew him and he went to some rich brat with hands like hunks of concrete.'

'Must have been some other pony, sir,' Paul said nervously, blinking and swaying from foot to foot because he was so tired, and Dora, wanting to support him without knowing what was up, said: 'I saw the Masons' pony jump. It was a much lighter chestnut, and not so –'

'Cobbler's Dream,' the Captain said. 'Did you steal him, boy?'

He fired it like a rocket, and Paul fired back: 'He's mine! I bought him. He's blind. He's got to be taken care of. If you won't do it, I'll find somewhere else.' Pushing past the Captain, he wrenched open the door of the stable and went in, fumbling to get the halter on the pony.

'Hold on,' the Captain said. 'I haven't said I won't take him. But you'll have to tell me the truth.'

Paul must have told him enough, for the Captain asked Tiny to put him to bed in the attic room that had been empty since William walked out in a sulk, and when he woke up twelve hours later, he offered him a job.

'What about his family?' Dora asked. 'You don't want them pounding down here in wrath and threatening to sue you because he's under age.' She looked at the Captain straight-faced, testing if it could be a joke, because it had happened with her parents and it had not been funny then, and since it was only six months ago, it might not be funny yet.

The Captain was not going to laugh before she did, but he winked at her with the eye that could – the other lid was stretched tight by the scar across the corner – to show her that he had recovered from the harangue and the table-thumping, and said: 'He'll be eighteen next month, and he invented the junk merchants. He has no family. The pony is a genuine case. His other eye will eventually go, there's no doubt, and the boy may as well stay too, if he can do the work. Don't narrow your eyes at me. You know we've been short-handed since William left unsung. A sixteen-year-old girl in red pants, a crumpled old man of seventy, a punch-drunk flyweight and that delinquent in the cowboy boots – what an outfit. My old Sergeant-major would die. You should be glad of a little new blood.' Dora did not say anything, so he added defensively: 'and at least he has a pair of jodhpurs.'

Dora put her hands in the pockets of the red slacks and looked up at him. 'Nothing to do with you not wanting to part the boy and the pony, I suppose?' she said bluntly.

Apart from being too short and too snub and too brown and healthy when everyone else was cultivating a sick indoors look of willowing pallor that drove the games mistress mad, it was Dora's bluntness that had excluded her from the paramount activities of the Grammar School seniors. Other girls said to the boys: 'You slay me, honest, you're a doll,' and: 'I'll bet you could sing on T.V. if you got a break.' Dora had said: 'If that's meant to be funny, I don't get it,' and: 'Is that singing or a soul in pain?'

The boys had ignored her. They had gone away and left her dateless in a generation whose little sisters were going steady and wearing rings. The Captain did not answer either. He walked away, but he turned on the cinder path that led from stables to the kitchen door and said: 'You should know by now – I'm not a sentimental man.'

This was a favourite expression, born perhaps of his dislike of the kind of fake sentiment he often met in his job. People who drooled over the veteran horses, crying: 'Poor fellow, what's the matter then?' to a contented old sway-back. The woman who had threatened him with a rolled umbrella when she came to see her decrepit old hunter after ignoring him for two years, and found him gone none too soon to the Elysian grazing.

Not a sentimental man, the Captain said, but of genuine sentiment he had a larger measure than he knew.

'And in any case,' he added, turning round again and seeing that Dora was still looking at him, 'I telephoned the man who used to own the pony, to check the story. He has the boy's money, so he can't do a thing, but he kept insisting that the pony should be put down, as if nothing else would satisfy him. Some sort of sour grape revenge, because he thinks the boy caused the injury.'

'Oh no!'

The Captain shrugged and walked on into the house, followed by the ugly little yellow mongrel with a broad flat muzzle like a hippopotamus, whom he had found as a dying puppy in a house of filth and despair, the very slums of hell.

On her way to start cleaning stables, Dora looked over the chestnut pony's door. Paul was grooming him, and the pony stood with one ear back and one ear forward, relaxed to enjoy it.

'Must have had better fitting harness than most junk dealers,' Dora said. 'No collar galls. No trace marks.'

'Told you Ginger was a pet, didn't I?' Paul kept his face away, pounding the pony's firm neck into satin.

'Don't bother with the Ginger stuff,' Dora said. 'The Captain told me everything.'

'He believe me?'

'He telephoned the man who used to own Cobbler's Dream and heard that your story was true.' As Paul turned in surprise, she realized that the Captain had possibly not meant to tell him. Ah well. Too late now. People should learn not to tell her their secrets.

'That's all he heard then.' It was neither a statement nor a question, elaborately casual.

'You mean – that the man thought you'd hit Cobby. Well, I don't believe it, and I'm sure the Captain –'

'Oh that.' The boy laughed through his nose, and turned back to the pony.

Ronnie Stryker, who came in from Town three miles away, was always late. He had slid away with it so far, because his uncle was the Captain's forage dealer, who made price concessions for a worthy cause, But if the worthy cause was to be not the horses, but the employment of the shock-haired nephew with the weaving walk, was it worth it?

'Who's this?' Ron demanded when he hurtled in on his motorcycle, scattering chickens and puppies, and found Paul on the feed barrow with Dora. Mincing in the boots that gave the Captain nightmares – but uncle or no uncle, it was not so easy to find boys or men to work in a stable these days – Ron approached Paul.

'Come to give us a hand, eh? Very nice of you, I'm sure. Much obliged.' He bowed to Dora, who made a gorilla face at him. 'Your servant, madam.'

Paul grinned briefly and took the hand that Ron held out, but drew it back quickly, for there was a tintack in the palm.

'Stryker's the name,' Ron said affably. 'Anything you want, just ask for me. They know me here.'

'They won't much longer,' Dora said, digging the measure into the grain and chaff mixture in the big wooden barrow, 'if you don't start mucking out. I've fed your side. For their sake, not for yours.'

'She's so yewmanitarian.' Ronnie stuck as much of his hands as he could get into the front pockets of his tight jeans, raised his shoulders to his ears and jazzed his feet a little, shadowed eyelids drooping, face blank as a wedge of processed gruyère. When Paul came out of Trotsky's stable with the empty feed tub, he shot at him through the match which was always between his lips: 'I seen that face before.'

'Not likely.' Paul went to the barrow and Ron bent to peer into his face, for the boy was shorter than he, though more solidly built.

'Funny,' Ron said, 'I never forget a face. Can't afford to, the way things are these days. Didn't you used to live in town?' He named a street near the canal, where the worst slums were. 'Remember the Bleeker Street raid? Remember the Roxy, the night they burned the screen?'

Paul shook his head. 'Not me.'

'Your living double then, Curly, though it was a year ago. Just shows you, don't it? I'd have sworn in blood I'd seen you around with the Hyena and his lot.'

Paul kicked open Mrs Berry's door and grunted at him sharply to get back, although the old roan with the mild, surprised face would fall over his cracked feet trying to get out of the way. He did not come out until Ron had moved off, whistling a blackbird phrase, and he did not talk any more to Dora; only to the horses.

Chapter Four

The Farm, whose oldest buildings went back three centuries, had been rebuilt as stables almost a hundred years ago when the national conscience was slowly awakening to the idea that charity might be applied to those who went on four legs, as well as two, and the R.S.P.C.A. was hounding the Government to strengthen the animal laws.

It was started as a convalescent home for the many horses who then worked on the steep and slippery streets of the manufacturing town, which crawled up the sides of the wide green valley like a spreading grey cancer. Falling sick through neglect or ignorance, injured in falls and street accidents, lamed by drivers to whom the horse was no more than the engine not yet invented to replace it, they came to the Farm for the care they could get nowhere else.

Veterinary surgeons were few, and too expensive for the underpaid carter, the street trader with his pony and barrow. For them there were only the quacks, horse doctors and cow-leeches, who had half a dozen crippling failures for every miracle cure.

When a horse was too far gone to work, he might be finished off by the pole-axe or the iron-headed mallet, lucky if the first blow fell true, hoofs slipping in panic on the blood of his fellows whose throats had already been cut – often before stunning – watched with idle interest by the children who lived in the rotting houses that overlooked the knacker's yard.

Or he might, when he was past work, simply go on working. The choice was not his to make, but if it had been, he might have chosen the slaughterhouse, with all its pain and terror. The men who administered the Farm for the rich old lady who founded it bought many stumbling, half-blind skeletons, mockeries of a horse's essential beauty, to give them the reward of a few months' or a few years' rest, and then, humanely, rest for ever.

The British are accused of being more sentimental about animals than about children, but in those passionless years of industrial progress when the old lady had the vision to endow her farm, few people were sentimental enough about either to care what was going on. Children had been freed from the mines, but they were still being used as cheap labour in factories and sweat shops. They were still being abused and half starved in institutions and schools to whom they were important only for the money that was paid for the board and education they did not get.

Children could not legally be sold, but there was good money in the export to the Continent of live horses – only just alive.

Old worn-out workers, many of them diseased and hopelessly lame, were stuffed into the holds of bucketing ships, packed like sardines to keep them upright. Half dead with a seasickness far worse than any human experience, since a horse cannot actually vomit, they were herded out on the docks of France or Belgium. Those who had not broken a leg on the nightmare crossing were then goaded to walk five miles or more to the abattoir, where they were killed with the knife, or the blunt hammer which did not always strike mercifully the first time.

There were Belgians living along the road who closed their shutters against the sight of these pitiable wrecks, shambling so meekly towards their death. The Veterinary College at Brussels often sent students to the docks at Antwerp, not to save the horses, but to observe them, since they had every imaginable disease and deformity.

On market days, especially after harvest, someone from the Farm would often bring back an old shire horse destined for export to save his winter keep. Or sometimes they would rescue a decrepit thoroughbred, or a broken-kneed hackney which had once stepped high and showy between the shafts of a Tilbury gig.

In those canting Victorian days of hour-long family prayers which had little expression in the lives of those who imposed them, a riding or driving horse was seldom a pet. When he was

29

past work, it was probably the groom's job to dispose of him. Since *Saucisson d'Anvers* was popular, the groom could get a higher price than the knacker's from a Belgian dealer, and pocket the extra.

The trade was so lucrative that it was not until 1950 that the export of live horses for slaughter was finally stopped, but they could still be legally exported from Ireland. Nearly a hundred years after those first decrepit refugees had come dot-and-carry into the brand new stables, to a humane death or a reprieve of quiet grazing, Mrs Berry rode in triumphantly in the back of a hired horse-box with the raw-boned roan she had bought at an Irish port.

They came out together, the horse and the brightly coloured little woman, holding on to his halter rope, as she had done throughout the journey for fear he might get claustrophobia if he was tied. She led him herself to his stable and wept gently over him as he dropped his ugly old head into the manger for his first feed.

He was a hideous animal, mottled slate and strawberry, with two inches of stiff erect mane which never grew any longer, a head like a clumsily-built coffin and a blank wall eye. Mrs Berry adored him. She had saved him from the guillotine, she said, and called him Evrémonde, but no one at the Farm ever called him anything but Mrs Berry.

She was so in love with the horse and what she had done for him that she was planning another trip to Ireland to bring back three more.

The Farm could not refuse them, since she had given money generously for years, and had handed over Evrémonde with an heiress's dowry. The Captain, however, did hint that when horses were brought up at the ports, the dealers usually supplied more, to keep the export number up and to keep the philanthropists happy.

Mrs Berry did not want to hear that. Throwing about her head and throat long pieces of the lavender material left over from her bedroom curtains, and grabbing, as they passed through the feed shed, a fistful of crushed oats to eat like toffees, she told the Captain he had the wrong spirit for his job and that if he had no room for her horses, he would have to build more boxes, and she would see about financing them when she had checked his spirit.

In the early days, the Farm had done a brisk business in holidays for the Town's horses and ponies. They came for two weeks to kick their heels at grass and blow the smoke out of their lungs. Many came back year after year, pulling their cart into the yard with ears eager. When they were turned out, they bucked and kicked and raced in mad thudding circles, crumpled down to roll, legs struggling like frantic beetles, grunted up to snort and shake, and then dropped stubby heads to graze, tearing at the grass like drunkards.

When a pony's two weeks were up, he would often be found near the gate of the long meadow, sensing that it was time to go; but you could not catch him. You could put your hand on him any day during the two weeks, but when his time was up, he might be by the gate, but it would take three men to corner him.

There were still a few coster ponies who came up the hill for a break each spring. Titch was a regular, and so was Taffy, the fat Welsh pony the colour of vanilla ice cream, who had every woman and child running out with biscuits and sugar as he went by with his cart of plants and bay trees and little pyramid firs, and who would never stand to wait unless his front feet were on the pavement.

But the town's working horses were few, and getting fewer. The brewery kept less than a dozen, and four of them were the chairman's coaching team, and pulled no barrels or bottles of beer. With the slums coming down and the new estates going up, the back alley stables and odorous sheds were disappearing too. You might have a cart and a licence to sell firewood, but you could not keep a pony on a council estate. A greengrocer had tried it once with a toolshed as camouflage, and been denounced by the neighbours – those who were not coming to him for manure.

Some of the displaced ponies were sold in the cattle market, and only God knew what became of them. Others came to the Farm. 'The stable's gone, see. I got a little van now, but I couldn't sell this chap. Been like a child to me, has Topper, good times and bad, and all the kids know him.'

The question was sometimes asked by visitors, and had been asked recently by the Animal Man of the region's television, who was going to include the Farm in a future show: 'Now that there is less cruelty to animals, and less horses anyway, why is this place always full? Hasn't the need for it somewhat disappeared?'

'There is always need,' the Captain said. 'Short of an accident, a horse can't usually work right up to the end.'

'You don't advocate then the, er –' throat cleared – 'humane killing of horses who are, let's say, past it?'

'Not unless they are suffering, or totally decrepit,' said the Captain in a voice that closed the subject. It was obviously not going to be discussed on children's television, and he was not going to discuss it now with the Animal Man, who seemed less an animal lover than a zoologist who had latched on to a good thing.

'Because there is less cruelty, he said more civilly, 'there are more voluntary inmates. The horses that came here in the old days were mostly rescued from people who could not have understood what the Farm was all about, even if they had heard of it. Many of our horses now come from good owners who feel the same way we do. They pay a bit if they can afford to, and they come and visit the old fellows.'

'It's an inspiring thing,' the Animal Man said, quite carried away, as he mentally jotted a few stirring lines for the script, 'that the dark old days are gone for ever, and man is at last enlightened enough to treat the beasts as brothers.'

So then the Captain took him out to see Prince, who had been found with his jaw tied to his fetlock, three days after he was stolen, and Nigger with the ruined mouth, the victim of the teenage Night Riders.

'There's a queer hard streak,' he said, 'a tradition of Midlands cruelty, that has never been broken. They've had it all: bull-baiting, bear-baiting, fighting cocks, cats skinned alive, crowds shrieking with joy as a dog and a monkey tore each other to bits. The Romans must have been here centuries back and taught them to lay bets on cruelty. If you knew the right people, you could go today to a cockfight, or a terrier hunt where the rats are bred to be let out under the noses of the dogs. Make a nice item for your programme. You could see mice made drunk enough to race, and half the folding part of a wage packet gambled away on them.'

'I knew a man once who used to race pieces of maggotty cheese across the table,' said the Animal Man, mildly smiling. But when they got to Prince's box, and then Nigger's, his smile was gone and so was his mildness. 'This goes on?' he asked, frowning the prawn eyebrows that the studio make-up girl wanted so badly to trim. 'These things are really happening?'

'Why not? It's part of the national disease. In the south they slash cinema seats. In the north they smash up railway carriages. Here they take it out on horses. That's why we bring ours in every night.'

The Animal Man was going to have to revise his script, or else not talk to the youngsters about their enlightened generation. He turned away from Nigger, baffled, and Ron Stryker, who had been mouthing and mugging behind his back like a ventriloquist's doll, said: 'Oh yes, it's shocking sir. It's really shocking.'

'Although I think,' the Captain said that evening in the farmhouse, 'that he knows more about it than he'll say. He probably even knows some of the gangs, eh boy?'

Paul shrugged and filled his mouth, but Tiny, passing behind him, nudged him with her powerful elbow, so that he was forced to say through baked apple so hot that the treacle was molten ore: 'How would I know?' And tried to make it sound both innocent and polite.

On Tiny's washing day, when she wrestled with wet sheets in the wind and boiled up great cauldrons of water laced with a vicious bleach that was the undoing of all but the stoutest fabric, they all ate supper in the stone-floored kitchen. On other days, the Captain sat formally with candles in the cold little dining-room, whether he had guests or not. He would have preferred the kitchen, but Tiny was afraid that he was going to seed from hanging about a stable all the time. As long as she had breath in her body to gasp her way along the passage with a loaded tray, she was not going to see things let go.

She had returned from a trip down to the village saying that she could not find a lodging for Paul, which was true in the sense that she had not even looked. There was something about the boy which seemed to claim her. It was the same quality that she had recognized in Slugger, when she scared the life out of him by announcing that they were going to be married. It was not helplessness. Paul was resilient and vigorous, and so had Slugger been in those early days. But there had been a suggestion of rootlessness, of drifting, as there was with Paul, a feeling that whatever was strong in his nature would only hold fast under guidance.

Slugger Jones, without knowing it, had called to Tiny to direct his life. Paul seemed a challenge too, and her protective strength was abundant. After her husband and the Captain and the fledglings and small wounded animals she rescued, there was enough left over for the son who would have been almost Paul's age if he had lived more than ten minutes after birth.

So Paul stayed on in the attic room with the wide brick chimney warming the whole end wall, and the gabled window showing him the stable-yard, with the corner box just in view, and the white-blazed perfection of the Cobbler's clever little head.

The square stone farmhouse with the steep roof and tall Tudor chimneys was set right at the top of the hill, looking down to the village directly below, and far beyond that, the darkening verges of the town. A frame of trees surrounded the house, so that from the valley, it looked like the other uninhabited clumps all along the range of hills. The people in the valley could not see the Farm, which did not trouble them, since it was too cranky an enterprise to be interesting, but the people at the Farm could see the smoky valley through a gap cut in the trees at the end of the front lawn. When the weather made her restless, Tiny would stand there with the Captain's field glasses, scanning the landscape like a storm-tossed Admiral, her skirts whipped flat to her strong legs and her short grizzled hair blown out like puppy's ears.

It was Tiny who had secured the job at the Farm, by selling herself as a housekeeper, which she had never been, rather than her husband as a stableman. Not that Slugger did not know quite a bit about horses, or had once, before a lot of it was pounded out of him, along with the few things he had picked

34

up at school, and the ability to communicate freely with his fellows.

He could still talk to horses, in a slow grumbling monotone which they seemed to find soothing. But to ask a question of anyone, he had to say: 'I wish I knew if ...' or: 'I wonder when he's going to tell me how ...' If he wanted to make a statement, it had to be: 'He'd ought to know ...' or: 'She'll find out that ...'

He was a small man with not much hair, slow-moving now, but very agile in his youth, when he was an apprentice at Newmarket. He was going to be a jockey then. He had wanted that all his life, but he got into boxing through the stable lads' tournament, and through boxing he got mixed up with Tiny.

She was a lady wrestler in those days, struggling and heaving in the matted ring with arms and thighs like iron, but when she fell in love with the bantamweight from Newmarket, he said that it was no place for a girl. She argued that she had stayed out of the mud, where some of her colleagues had made crude success, but Slugger said that when he heard a body go thwack on the mat, he did not want it to be his girl's.

Tiny gave in, because he was her first love, and it had stunned her; but she quickly came to, and it was the last time he ever had the final say. She was boxing mad, so he gave up his apprenticeship at the stables for the professional ring. He had some small success, but he was never as good as she thought he was. By the time he was slugged out, with a thick ear and teeth broken diagonally across a childlike mouth, he was not fit enough or sensible enough to start riding again.

So Tiny sat down in the red velour armchair which was with her now at the Farm, because she was taller than he, and if she sat down while he stood, it gave the illusion of a discussion on an equal level. He could not box, he could not ride, but he knew how to take care of horses. She was a shocking cook, and her passage with a broom distributed more dust than it collected, but married couples were in demand, and who would take on Slugger on his own in this state? Who indeed? He smiled round the broken teeth with a sweetness that rebuked all the fists that had smashed into that gentle mouth.

'She can't cook for toffee though,' Tiny heard him mutter as she got up, and she whipped round, sweeping a cup and saucer off the dresser with her arm like a violent-tailed dog clearing off a cocktail table.

'I can learn, can't I?'

They had found the job at the Farm, and she had learned on the Captain.

Uncle Dick Catchpole, who was older than most of the horses if you calculated the life span proportion, had been at the Farm far longer than Slugger, and had tolerated two managers before the Captain. He and his wife could scarcely remember when he was not there, that far-off time when he drove a horse tram from Hooker's Mill to the Town Hall, via Commercial Street and Bald's Hill – with a trace horse.

When one of the tram horses fell, 'a wet, foul night it was, with the Christmas crowds on the loose,' Uncle would recall nearly fifty years later, with the same inspired surprise as if he were telling it for the first time, 'a chap come up with a gun and offered to shoot poor Jim dead for nothing.'

'For the good of the horse, he says, and all the passengers standing about gaping as if they'd not had it in mind to go any farther than to see this spectacle anyway. 'For the good of the horse,' I says, somebody get me a knife so I can cut the poor beggar loose from his harness and give him a chance to get up.

'We unhitched the other horse – Rosie her name was, after the horsekeeper's wife; he'd call all the horses after different ones in his own family. Then someone run into a butcher's shop and we cut old Jim loose, but we couldn't get him up, and we *couldn't* get him up, and here's the gun still cocked and it turns out the chap on the trigger end of it is on the board of the Tram company. I knew the old horse was all right, just wanting strength, so we was pulling with ropes, and a hup! hup! and when I see the chap take aim, I get between Jim and the gun, and he's bawling at me and I'm bawling at him and the passengers is bawling for the pure love of it . . .'

Here he would lose the narrative, and those seasoned, like Dora, to listen, would ask the appropriate question.

'Ah, you may well ask what came of it. I lost me job and so did the horse. When we finally get him on his feet, the chap still thinks the leg is broke, for he's dangling it, but I won't have

36

it, for 'tis the string of the muscle is gone, and in a bit, he puts it to the ground like an old maid trying hot bathwater.

'They tell me: "Walk him to the knackers, and keep on walking, you." So I did, and so did Jim. It took him half-a-day and half-a-night to come them four miles here, but he lived to tell the tale and died of old age ten years after, much loved by all and a favourite with the visitors on account of this little trick he had of seeming to count with his hoof what number you said, one, two, three.'

'But of course,' Dora told Paul, who was hearing the story for the first time, 'Uncle was going psst, psst, psst, to make him.'

'Be daft if I weren't,' Uncle said, 'for there weren't the horse born that could figure the count for hisself. But the visitors didn't rumble me, because they were looking for marvels, and when that old grey horse counted – a lady asks for twenty-two once and I nearly lost my teeth – they had to put as many pennies in the collection box.'

'Pity we can't teach Nero to hold his mouth open for pennies instead of sugar, and spit them out,' Paul said.

'Nero,' said the old man, sniffing his blue-black lips up under his nose. 'He's never give up doing that to one and all since that chap with the slipper shoes come for the Christmas calendar and used two pound of sugar lumps to get the picture right. No art in that. But old Jim now, that was something else.'

In the front room of the cottage which stood in the field across the road from the stables, surrounded by grazing horses, there was a browned picture of the square grey horse with Uncle at his head, bleaching inwards from the edges. Over it, Uncle's daughter had lettered in three colours: 'Good-bye Faithful Friend.'

Dora lived at the cottage with Uncle and Mrs Catchpole, who was never called Aunt, except by her sister's children. She was a speckless, starched old lady, shrunk from a lifetime's laundering, neckless and pottering like some small field animal in aprons. Although her experience had been narrow, and she had moved only once, from the town to the Farm, and never been to London, she had a broad tolerance which excused everything, from Ron Stryker's small excesses to the ghastliest news of massacre abroad as: 'It's just their way.'

When Dora's mother first saw her, she felt better about Dora having this impossible job, too young away from home. But when she got home, to the crenellated villa where her husband gave his violin lessons and she and Desmond the play-readings and group talks for the Outlook Club, she began to search her soul.

What have I done? Have I failed Dossie in some way? Running away to the stables, that I couldn't help, for it's been in her like malaria ever since she knew the difference between a horse and a cow. But why is she happy in that stuffy little cottage – that front window hasn't been opened for years; it's painted up – when she never was at home with all she had? She doesn't look sulky any more. Her mouth is a different shape. Is this then what I should have been – a little old lady in half glasses murmuring: 'It's only her way,' as she picks up the towels and clothes from the floor and scrapes manure off the shoes?

Manure. The child stank of horses, and that was a fact. All the heartache and anxiety over whether the Grammar School would take her since her father was on the staff – what a long time ago that seemed, and what good had come of it in the end? She had only waited until the law allowed her to leave, and then away up the hill to the horses, where she had always wanted to be, and all her mother's careful years of trying to rationalize her into the kind of person her brother was, gone like a dandelion seed.

'It was a shock to them at home,' Dora told Paul, 'but a bigger shock to the Captain, because he'd forgotten saying: "Come back when you've left school," to get rid of me when I followed him around asking him questions.'

'He's not sorry now, I'll bet,' Paul said gallantly, and because she was not a girl to whom people said gallant or complimentary things, she frowned, which was what she did instead of blushing, and said: 'I do a man's work, don't I?'

'He doesn't like girls in a stable though,' she told him when they were taking Dolly and the cart out with new rails for the fence in the bottom field. 'He had to let me in because he'd promised, but he wouldn't take another, although they're much easier to get than men. Boys don't like horses any more. Girls like them better than they ever did. Why is that? The Captain says they're in revolt from the age of machinery they don't want to understand.'

She was always quoting the Captain. It was irritating, so Paul said scornfully: 'Him too. He drives that little car as if he was afraid it was going to buck him off. He'd want to go back to the days of this, I suppose.' He slapped the reins on Dolly's sunken back, and she dreamed on, no faster, no slower.

'He's not that old. He's not as old as he looks. He isn't even fifty.'

'That's half as old as God.' When he was a child, Paul had often heard his mother, dressed to go out, adoring herself in the mirror, vow that she would gas herself if she ever looked like being fifty. She must be over forty now though, wherever she was. Time to stop talking like that. 'Why's he only a Captain then?' he asked Dora.

'Something happened in the Army, they say. I don't know. Perhaps not. Tiny's got it all muddled up. Perhaps he's been in prison.'

'So what?' Paul said quickly, and Dora said: 'Oh nothing,' and frowned. 'I didn't mean – I'm not smug like that, minding what people have done. At home they said I had no ethics. But the Captain sometimes looks – I don't know – lonely and sad, with that scar pulling at the corner of his eye. Old Doll did that, you know.' She threw a toffee paper at the mare's bony rump. 'Any place else but the Farm, anyone else but the Captain, she wouldn't be here to tell the tale.'

'What did she do?'

'She'd been so badly treated, she thought all men were enemies. The Captain was leading her out to grass, because no one else could handle her, and she suddenly whipped the rope through his hands and got her back end to him. It never healed right. He didn't go to the doctor soon enough. It was before Tiny came, or she'd have made him go. She'd have made him shoot Dolly too, she says, but he wouldn't have. He would never think of putting a horse down for a little thing like laying open the side of his head. It isn't their fault. The Captain believes that everything a horse does is conditioned by people. A wild horse hasn't got a character, he says. Only instincts. They get their personalities from people. It's all put into them, the good and the bad. Doll's forgotten now what she had against men, but she's still better with me than anyone else.'

'Why do you cut your hair so short?' Paul asked, without looking at her. 'Are you one of those horrible girls who wish they'd been born boys, and try to look like them?'

'I've got two skirts,' Dora said angrily, for in her childhood she had led a secret life for years under the name of Donald. 'And my hair gets full of hay seeds and horse dust. I have to wash it all the time. Don't you like it like this?' She asked it straight, not knowing how to be coy.

Paul grunted. 'Colour's not too bad.'

'Because it's like Cobby's. I know.' She jumped down to open the gate between the fields, to let Dolly and the cart lurch through the mud that many horses had trampled impatiently, waiting to come in for the evening feed.

Chapter Five

Cobbler's Dream made a big hit on television. He did so well that Uncle, who never fully recognized a horse until it had been at the Farm at least a year, said that it were not good enough, and hid in Flame's stable at the end when the staff were supposed to be lined up with the Captain, smiling humanely and looking dedicated.

The old man was upset because the Animal Man would not bring the camera down to Flame's end box. She was the oldest horse there, except for Charley the pit pony, and the blood of champions ran in the veins that seamed her narrow head and spare stiff shoulders.

'Too thin,' the Animal Man had said. 'If we show her, you'll have half the country telephoning to complain you starve the horses.'

'Let em,' said Uncle, who would not have to answer the telephone. 'If they don't know a thoroughbred is always thin, bad luck to em. Feel er skin, feel er skin now, man.' He laid a gentle horned hand on the mare's lean neck. 'Like a lady's glove. Where are you going to find anything like that? The skin of a thoroughbred.'

'Yes but,' said the Animal Man, who did not want to spend time with the broken-kneed old racehorse when there were so many other more colourful subjects, 'they aren't going to *feel*, you know. They're going to see. And this one – well, she's not exactly a good advertisement for your care, let's face it.'

He had not wanted to hurt Uncle, but he did. Having satisfied himself that this man with the quick bird movements and the sheepskin hair neither understood, nor wanted to understand, anything about old horses who had faithfully served their time, Uncle stayed in the background disguised as a wheelbarrow and would not appear on camera, to the undying chagrin of his daughter, who had assembled her husband's relations from three countries to witness his glory.

The camera passed along the line of boxes, with the Captain introducing each horse. He had expected to enjoy being on television, and showing off his horses to what he was assured was an audience of thousands. 'Parents as well as kids. It's the family supper hour. Great time for viewing. They stick the set at the head of the table and it saves bothering to talk.'

He had been into town for a close haircut and an eyebrow trim, so as not to be identified with the unmilitary luxuriance of the Animal Man, and had bought himself, if not a new jacket, at least new leather pieces for Tiny to stitch on to the elbows and cuffs of the old one. But when the time came, and his neat cobbled yard was a tangle of cables and improbably young technicians, he was suddenly afraid, and became very British and tongue-tied, like a Guards officer called upon to describe his wife.

'Not a bad mare ... had it tough ... fair shape now ... rather sad story there – er yes. What? Oh – er, usual thing, you know.'

The little speeches he had practised with the Animal Man were choked away and swallowed, and when they came to the Cobbler, white blaze a-dazzle, nostrils wide, ears taut as bow-strings for the commotion in the yard, Paul stepped up un-summoned to do his pony justice.

With Ron Stryker mopping and mowing at him like a de-mented marionette from behind the cameras, Paul told the Animal Man that Cobbler's Dream had once jumped six feet, which Dora knew was a lie, since Paul had told it to her as five feet six, which meant it was more like five.

'Who was on him?'

Paul stuck out his boxy chest in the tight polo sweater, which Tiny had favoured with her special laundry treatment. 'He's won prizes in the show ring for these kids, yes. Nothing to touch him when he was properly ridden. But he'd never jump really big for anyone but me.'

Self-exuberance goes down better on the screen than in the flesh, so the camera was held on Paul, and he was asked to bring the Cobbler out for admiration.

'He really jump that high?' the Animal Man asked, for the Cobbler was not much more than fourteen hands.

'Yes sir. I'd have tackled anything on him. You get that – that you know – that sort of squeeze and lift as if you were doing the whole thing yourself, but in your mind more than in your body, you –' Crouching a little, with his elbows out and his arms tense, Paul threw the heart and spirit of himself over an imaginary jump, as high as the barn roof.

'He's a grand pony.' The Animal Man turned from Paul's enthusiasm with a smile and addressed his lecturing face to the dispassionate one-eyed stare of the camera.

'You see the combination of power and grace. The short-coupled back, the fine legs, the clever little head. Good points to judge your horse by,' he told his supper-table audience, most of whom would never get closer to possessing a horse than sixpennorth of its time at Whitsun fair. 'Frankly,' he said, slapping Cobby on his gleaming muscular neck, 'he doesn't look as if he ought to be here.'

'Blind.' The Captain jerked his head aside, as he remembered too late Dora's orders to keep his unscarred profile to the camera. 'One eye gone and the other going.'

'Not yet,' Paul said quickly. He would not consider the day when the Cobbler would not be able to see at all. 'He don't miss a thing. Give us a kiss then, Cobb.'

The pony put his nose up to the boy's curly hair and lipped his black head all over, nuzzling. When he dropped his head down to his hand, Paul spoke to him in a sing-song murmur without words, and the pony fluted his nose in the small confiding sounds the boy was imitating.

'Talking to horses, eh?' the Animal Man said. 'Does he understand everything you say?'

'Point is,' Paul looked up, squinting unselfconsciously into the sun that squatted on the ridgepole of the barn roof, as if he had forgotten camera, crew, and supper-table audience, 'I try to understand what he says. Most people, they'll tell you about an animal: "He understands everything I say." All right, is a horse smarter than a man? If he was, he'd never be broke. It makes more sense for us to understand them, sooner than expect them to learn to understand us.'

'By God,' said the Captain surprised, 'the boy's right, you know,' but the headphoned producer, shackled with a dozen wires in the middle of the yard, was making time signals at the Animal Man, who smiled: 'It's fascinating,' and moved towards the next box.

Behind his back, Paul said quietly: 'Give us a ride then, Cobb,' and the pony put his head between his legs, lifted, and slid the boy down his strong neck on to his back.

'Taught himself that,' Paul said gaily, and slid down over the chestnut tail. The camera left him, reluctantly, to pick up the yellow coffin head of the Mongolian pony who had come from Siberia years ago with a load of pit props, and within an hour, five of the people, who would have protested about Flame's ribs, had telephoned to complain that Cobbler's Dream was taught tricks by cruelty.

They did not telephone about Nero, because it was obvious that he was self-taught, from greed. He never bothered to perform for the staff, who were immune to his plea, but as soon as a stranger came near his door, he would thrust his head out sideways, jaws wide as an alligator, for lumps of sugar to be thrown into the cavern of his jagged old back teeth. He was still doing it long after the Animal Man and the camera had passed on down the line, until a technician threw in a pebble when no one was looking, and Nero closed his mouth with a clack and drew in his head.

The donkeys from Blackpool were shown, and the camera focused on the crucifix stripe down the back and shoulders, in case anyone had never seen a donkey. Then came the mule which had been found in the canal one night by a man who had gone there to drown himself, but became so interested in the mule's rescue, with ropes and tractors, that he only remembered after he had gone home to dry his feet what it was he had come out for.

'This is a female mule,' the Animal Man said, pulling at one of Willy's long, muscular ears. 'A jennet, or henny, they call them. Her mother was a Jenny donkey and her father was a horse. Isn't that right, Captain?'

The Captain nodded, although Willy was actually a male, by a Jack donkey out of a mare, but he had not been listening.

Cobby had got his foot caught in a cable as he turned to go into his stable. Another horse would have pulled back hysterically, tightening the check and doubling the trouble. Cobby stood quietly while Paul disentangled him, then walked into his box with a roll of his round quarters, his long bright tail swinging like a bell.

The bay police horse went through his act of standing stolidly with his eyes half closed and his ears lopped out sideways while Dora opened a red umbrella at him, and Ron let off a firework under his mealy nose. The story was told of the brewery horse who had saved her driver when the young horse teamed with her had bolted. She had to gallop with him, but she had forced him to the right side of the road, charging against him to turn left at the corners, until they skidded to a stop in the brewery yard, with the young horse sitting down and scraping all the hair off his tail.

The programme was a little too cosy for the Captain's liking. Everybody was doing a wonderful job. Every horse was charmingly at peace. If he had had his way, he would have stressed the point, not of present content, but of past suffering. He would have liked to say that many of them would not be here if it were not for human cruelty, persisting stubbornly, as if no shaft of light had ever come to the Dark Ages. He would have liked to show Prince and Nigger, and show what happened when you tried to touch Nigger's head, and talk about the Night Riders and the fantastic, witless savagery of boys who would destroy anything, living or inanimate, in their restless search for thrills.

The Animal Man, however, did not want to be involved in anything so basic. Let the magazine programmes handle that. This was a children's show, worthily designed to teach the young how to treat animals. If you showed kindness, they would copy kindness. If you showed violence, they might be tempted to copy that. There was too much violence on television anyway, the Animal Man had said, during a brisk, though civilized argument at rehearsal. Had not the Captain himself told him that the Night Riders were inspired by Westerns?

So by the end of the programme, the Captain was a little fed up. When Dora, in lipstick and a sharply pressed pair of

45

slacks, brought out the two Shetland ponies and stood with her arms round their stubby necks, which she had to bend down to do, he said: 'The little one, the piebald, he shouldn't be here at all. Nothing wrong with him, except that some fool woman tried to keep him in a big dog kennel and found that he wasn't a dog. He'll have to go, if we can find a decent home for him.'

The rashest words he ever spoke. In the next day's mail, there was not only a letter from the dog-kennel woman's solicitor, referring to 'matters defamatory to my client's reputation', but three dozen offers, on postcards, notepaper, and pages torn from exercise books, of a home for the Dear little black and white pony we saw on T.V. And that was only the beginning. After one more day, three reporters had come with cameras, and the post office van was unloading mail by the sackful. 'Had to make an extra trip out,' the postman told the Captain. 'You want to be more careful what you say.'

Chapter Six

Over the fireplace at the brick and flint cottage hung a large photograph of a horse, accoutred for steeplechasing, and the man on his back was in quartered colours and jockey cap.

It was not the only picture of either the man or the horse in the room, and the corner cupboard was stuffed with trophies; but it was the last picture ever taken of them together. The horse was big and rangy, with the head of a genius and the eye of a saint. The man, turning with half a smile for the camera, was firm-chinned, with a full, tolerant mouth and a steady gaze. Neither the man nor the horse looked as old as they were when the picture was taken, after they ran second at Newbury. The horse was twenty and the man was forty-eight.

Callie, who was twelve, with a smooth brown fringe roofing her eyes and narrow pigtails at the back of her small round head, stood on a chair and lifted the photograph carefully off the nail. She felt that she ought to be crying. But you didn't always cry at the things that hurt the most. You cried for trivial things, like not getting a part in the Christmas play, or watching a crowded bus sail past you in the rain. The big things, like being reminded that your father was dead and the horse which had been a part of him condemned, needed something graver than the ordinary kind of tears that anyone can shed.

Clutching the picture to her chest, Callie went into the front room, where her mother was packing books into a deep cardboard box.

'I suppose *she* won't let us hang this, up at the house,' she said truculently.

'Darling.' Anna Sheppard sat back on her heels and pushed aside a lock of soft pale hair. 'Jean isn't a monster. It's going to be our home, just like before. She isn't going to make serfs of us.'

'She will though.' Callie put the picture across the arms of a shabby chair and sat down opposite, chin in hands, elbows on spread knees, staring. 'She's never going to let us forget it's her house now, you'll see. First Peter was hers, and then the house, and now he's letting her do this terrible thing to Wonderboy.'

'Don't,' her mother said. 'Don't talk about her like that. I'm sure she doesn't want to live with us any more than we want to live with her. But it does seem as if she knows what's best for all of us. Amazing, a young girl like that. When I was her age, I was still in a tree house, reading Shelley. But she's so practical. It's about time we had someone like that in this family.'

'I don't see why.' Callie's chin ground into her cupped hands. 'We were happy before. A lot happier than we are now.'

'That's nothing to do with Jean and you know it,' Anna bent forward into the depths of the box and began to push books about down there, squaring them up fussily without seeing them. 'We can't expect to be as happy as we used to be.'

'Shan't we ever be happy again?' Callie asked, and her mother left the box and came to her in one long swift movement and they clung together, crouched in the chair, while opposite them the man sat proudly in the small racing saddle, stirrups short, hands relaxed, his face alive with the pleasure of what the big brown horse had done.

It had only been six months after the race that John Sheppard had died during an operation. It was quite unpredictable, quite unavoidable. Nothing could have been done to prevent it, they said. His heart had failed, and he had died, and his wife and children were left with the irony that he need never have had the operation on his knee. He had walked with a slight limp for years.

He owned a small paint factory outside the town, and had lived all his life on the farm five miles away, where his father had raised Herefords before he bought the factory, which he left to John.

When John died, somewhere within the fastnesses of the grey archaic hospital, the paint factory was Peter's – and the debts and mismanagement that went with it.

'Too much time in the saddle and not enough in the office,' it was said when it was revealed how little there was going to be for the family after the taxes were paid. But things were different now. His son did not ride. At twenty-two, Peter, who was engaged to a crisp, glossy girl with decorated glasses like devil's eyes, set his cogs going for the long grind up to where the factory might show a profit.

He married Jean quickly, not only because she was the kind of wife a successful businessman should have, but because he was lonely for his father. He had never been very close to his mother. He had always been a conventional boy, reading books appropriate to his age, scrupulous of rules, wearing the right clothes for the right sport and the right season. He was often baffled by his mother's gentle blend of naïveté and shrewdness, and the 'crank ideas' which he was afraid that Callie was absorbing. They both argued with him about shooting, and he had caught Anna with a leaflet from the anti-blood-sport people. Thank God his father had never known about that!

Peter and Jean did not turn Callie and her mother out of the low, shadowy house with the stone mullions and the spotless, empty, useless dairy. They took themselves away to the newer cottage by the stables, where there had once been six horses, and then only two, and now only the old steeplechaser Wonderboy. Most of the farmland had been sold long ago, but there was still a good paddock behind the stables. After a year, when things were going worse instead of better, Jean said that they should sell the cottage and all be together at the big house. 'It's the sensible thing to do,' she said. If something were only sensible enough, it must be possible to fit people into its design.

No one wanted the cottage with the leaky roof and sunken door sills, but a fair price was offered by a goat breeder for the cottage, stables and paddock together. Jean said that they would be mad not to accept. Wonderboy? He was so old already that it would be the right and proper thing to have him put down.

She said this at a family conference, one of the many dismal discussions they had held since John Sheppard died, in the low central hall with the yielding sofas and chairs, where Callie had spent a large part of her childhood winters on the bench inside the fireplace, scorching the toes of her shoes in the hot ash.

'If you kill Wonderboy,' Callie had said, with the hatred in her heart sharpening her voice to steel, 'it will be like killing one of us.'

'Let's be practical.' Jean crossed her long beautiful legs smoothly and admired her narrow foot. She was always saying things like that: Let's be practical. Let's look at it squarely. Let's be adult about this thing. Who wanted to be adult? 'Peter is the head of the family now.' She smiled at Mrs Sheppard to show that she was not trying to domineer. 'It's up to us to back him up in what he's trying to do. Things will get better. They're bound to, because he's tackling this the right way. But meanwhile, we've got to help him all we can. I've got my job, little enough though it is,' she dissembled sweetly, though she privately thought that her work at the Town Hall was more important than the factory. 'And if you can really get a typing job, Anna, we'll manage. But we've got to cut down on everything. No extras. You've told me yourself, Callie, Wonderboy can't just be turned out to grass. He needs oats, bedding, hay, shoeing bills.' Although she was proud to be strictly out of the horse world, she had familiarized herself somewhat with its economics. 'Even if we could afford to keep him, there will be nowhere for him next month after the goat people move in.'

'I hate them,' Callie said.

'You haven't even met them.' Jean went on without looking at her: 'Anyway, Peter agrees with me. It was his suggestion, not mine.' She looked at her husband to support her, because although she could not help trying to take over his hopeless family, she wanted them to like her, as everybody must like her, if she was to be a success.

'Look.' Peter leaned forward, trying to make some contact with his mother, who was sitting stone-faced, moving only her eyes, guarding her thoughts. 'I know how you feel about old Boy. I feel the same way too.' He was temporarily emotional enough to believe it, although he had always been the one who was not interested in the horses, and resented the time and money and besotted attention given to them. 'He's the only horse in the world, and he and Dad – well, they were really famous in their way, I suppose, keeping at it for so long . . .'

'Your father was not in his dotage, you know,' Anna said gently.

'You know I didn't mean that.' Peter hitched his long neck round in his office collar. 'I meant Boy. He's in his dotage, for a horse. He's lame now, and he can't have much longer to live. It truly would be kinder to de—' He substituted: 'put him to sleep,' seeing Callie's pinched face.

'He's as fit as ever he was,' the child said grimly, crouching on the sofa like a miserable moulting bird. 'Dad gave him to me. You know he once said in a joke: "When I die, you can have anything of mine you want most." He's mine. I want to keep him.'

'Darling –' her mother said, but Callie drew away from her arm along the sofa, and Jean said: 'Poor baby. We do understand. We'll never forget him, will we? I'll have a paper-weight made for you out of his hoof.'

'And a third pigtail for her made out of his tail!' Anna cried, jumping up and tipping a drably striped cat out of her lap. 'How can you Jean? How can you be like that? I hope you never have children!'

'What have I done now?' Jean turned the hard swoop of her glasses to Peter with another stock phrase and a face of aggrieved innocence after Anna and Callie had run out.

As soon as they were outside in the dark, Anna had stopped on the path that led round the side of the house, leaned her head against a crusty espaliered pear, and wailed: 'What a wicked thing to say! How can you bear me to be so mean?'

In the evening, when the things that were to go up to the house were packed, and the small rooms of the cottage echoed round the few bits of furniture that were to be left for the goat breeder, Jean came in at the front door. Everyone else had always come round by the back, but Jean used the front door, letting in an overwhelming smell of pinks from the musky May garden.

'You're having supper with us,' she told Anna. 'No, of course you must. You've hardly got anything to cook with.'

'We have a pie to finish.'

'Let the dogs have it. Look here, why don't you move in tonight to sleep? This is depressing.'

'Our beds are like islands in lakes of floor,' Anna said. 'It's Callie's last night here.'

'It's like a tomb.'

It had been their tomb. Their refuge where they had been alone together with their sorrow, and together had begun slowly to burn into life again, each kindling sparks in the other.

'I promised her tonight.'

'You're mad,' Jean said pleasantly. 'Where is she?'

'Feeding Wonderboy. Perhaps she will finish up the grain bin on him and kill him off that way.'

Jean drew her dark eyebrows down below the broad frame of her glasses. Although she was not very shortsighted, she never took them off and allowed her face to be vulnerable. She said warily: 'You agreed, you know. You're not going back on it?'

'Oh *no*,' Anna said ingenuously. 'But Callie and I are just going to ask the goat man – not press it, just mention it casually – if we can have the use of one loose box – just for a while.'

'Honestly, there's no end to it. Doesn't anybody ever face anything in this family? You'll only make it worse for Callie in the end.'

'We were just going to ask the man, that's all,' Anna said with the questionable humility which infuriated her daughter-in-law, because she could not quite prove that it was faked. 'He can always say no.'

Callie came in, stamping manure off her shoes on the door-sill.

'We're going up to the house for supper,' her mother said, 'so go and put on a skirt.'

'A skirt!' It might have been a straitjacket. Then the horror left her face. 'They're all packed.'

As they went out of the cottage and her mother stopped and bent down to cup her hand under the flowerhead of a tiny plant, Callie said in her ear: 'Don't let it be skirts for supper from now on. Remember it was our house first.'

Waiting for supper, Callie wandered restlessly about the shadowy hall, touching things, knocking into furniture, confronting with stony contempt the pictures that had been put up since her day. She kept clutching her stomach and saying: 'I'm hungry.'

'I'm not ready yet,' Jean said, collecting ashtrays. Why didn't she empty them into the fireplace? It would all get burned up next autumn.

'Can I turn on the television?' Callie asked, and when her mother told her to go to the kitchen and ask Jean, she said: 'When we're living here, do I have to ask her everything?'

Her mother looked at Peter, and Peter turned out his hands and pulled his jaw down and sideways, in a flabbergasted grimace he had picked up years ago at school and never lost. 'Don't drag me into it,' he said. 'You girls are going to have to work this out between you.'

'The thing I cannot understand,' Callie said for the twentieth time, as her mother bent over the bed, which revealed its true ugliness shipwrecked in the middle of the bare dormer room, 'the thing I absolutely fail to understand is why I never thought of it before.'

'We,' Anna said. 'I knew about that place too. It's been there as long as I can remember.'

'One of those horses was forty,' Callie said. 'Wonderboy will have years of peace before he has to die. Tell me again what that man said.'

'No kind of beast is there on earth, nor fowl that flieth with its wings, but is a folk like you. Then unto their Lord shall they be gathered.'

Callie's eyes were closed, but when Anna was at the door, she sat up suddenly, staring and tense. 'Suppose they won't take him! Suppose they haven't got room for Wonderboy!'

'There's still our idea about the goat man.'

'We never believed he'd agree. It was just something we told each other so as not to give up hope.'

'On Saturday,' Anna Sheppard said. 'We'll go to the Farm on Saturday.'

It was not like they thought it would be. On the television show, it had all seemed so well-ordered, with everyone walking about calmly, knowing their job and using quiet, confident voices. When Anna and Callie left the shabby little car by the

53

gate and walked with eager diffidence under the stone arch, they met mild chaos.

Two photographers and a small child with starched petticoats and ribbons in her hair were at one side of the yard with the Shetland pony, trying to get a picture without Dora holding the halter rope. But as soon as she gave the rope to the little girl and let go, the pony knocked the child aside and charged head down across the yard, scattering women and a group of Brownies with crusts of stale bread in paper bags.

Uncle was standing in the doorway of the hay barn with a pitchfork at alert like a pike, shouting at a reporter, because the reporter thought he was deaf and was shouting at him. The yard was full of visitors. Nero was waving his open mouth back and forth like a demented crocodile, and several horses were banging on their doors, for the output of titbits was phenomenal.

'We shouldn't have come.' Callie drew back against her mother. 'We should have telephoned. There's too many people. They'll never bother about us.'

'Courage,' said her mother. She stood against the wall in a characteristic attitude, with her small pale head poked forward and her soft doe's eyes scouting ahead for her. 'Who shall we tackle, do you suppose?'

They held hands for a moment, and then decided on Dora, but as they started towards her, the pony broke free again, and Dora plunged after it, shouting schoolgirl abuse.

Slugger Jones came out of a stable, with the tweed fishing hat pulled down over his battered ears.

'Please –' said Anna. 'What's going on?'

'What's going on, she wants to know.' Slugger stopped to rub a finger along the broken ridge of his nose. 'She should read the papers, that's what she should do.'

He stood with bent head, dropping words into a small round drain in the ground, and when Anna asked him whom she might see about bringing a horse, he told the drain: 'A horse. A horse, she says. She wants to bring us a horse,' and walked on.

Callie was looking at the horses, going from door to door, recognizing ones she had seen on television. Ronnie Stryker was in the donkeys' stable with a mouthful of nails, hammering at the manger. When Callie stood on tiptoe to look in, since the donkeys were too small to put their heads over the top of the door, Ronnie looked up and winked and said: 'Want to buy a donkey? It's all you need.'

'Actually,' Callie said, straining to keep her chin on top of the high half door, 'we've come here to ask if you could possibly take our old horse. You do let people bring horses here, don't you?'

'Horses?' Ronnie stood upright and took all the nails out of his mouth but one. 'Oh ňo, dear. I shouldn't think so.'

'But then, how did they all – I mean –?'

'Oh no.' He shook his top-heavy head solemnly. 'We don't take *horses* here. Whatever gave you that idea?'

'You're joking,' Callie said uncertainly.

'Wish I was.' Ronnie put the nails back in and hitched at his tight trousers so that he could bend again to the low manger. 'Wish I had time to make jokes,' he mumbled through the nails. 'Wish I had as much time to make jokes as some kids has to ask soppy questions.'

Callie let her weight down on to her heels, disconsolate, and looked round for her mother. She could not see her, but she saw the long white blaze of the pony Cobbler's Dream over the corner door, and went to him and blew down her nose into his nose to see if he would like her. He suffered it for a while, then flung up his head and curled his top lip backwards over his strong yellow teeth.

Callie laughed. 'That's what Wonderboy used to do when my father blew cigarette smoke at him,' she told the pony.

'You been smoking too much then,' Paul said at her elbow. 'You like the Cobbler?'

'Oh yes. I saw him on television. And you too, of course.' She blushed, for to her the boy was now a famous figure.

'Wasn't he something? I reckon he's made for life. They'll be sending for him from Hollywood. All that fuss about the Shetland. Useless little brute. Might as well have a lapdog. At least that wouldn't kick as well as bite.'

'Is that what all the fuss is about?' Callie asked.

'Dead right. Ever since the programme, it's been murder. People coming in droves. It's mad. They could go to the sales and buy twenty ponies better than that one, but what the Captain said about having to find a home for Mickey – that tugged at their heartstrings. Like the commercials. If they see it on the telly, they want it. And when it got into the papers – good night.'

'Actually,' Callie confided, glancing over her shoulder to see if her mother could hear, for she had not told even her this, 'I was going to ask if I could have him, though we haven't got a stable now.'

'In the toolshed, I suppose.'

Callie nodded, biting the end of her hair. 'How did you –'

'That's what they all say. About half the people who come to rescue Mickey don't realize there's more to a pony than brushing its mane and feeding it carrots. One woman asked me if I thought she could keep it in her flat, as there was a service lift at the back.'

'I'm too late then,' Callie said. 'I thought he was unwanted.'

'Unwanted? You should see the letters the Captain's got. Stacks and stacks of 'em and still coming. He says he's going to read them all, but the thing's ridiculous. He'll keep his mouth shut next time. Only there won't be a next time. He's had it.'

'Is he angry?' Callie searched the boy's clear blue eyes with her own, in which points of green and grey light flickered. 'Will he mind, do you think, if I ask him whether he could take our poor old horse?'

'He's never minded yet, as far as I know. He's a sucker for a sad story.'

'Then perhaps he'll take Boy.' Callie felt her mouth stretching into a smile, and realized that she had not smiled since she and her mother came nervously into the yard. Too much had been at stake; there was no room for smiling. 'Wonderboy. You might have heard of him. He's a famous steeplechaser.'

'Don't follow the races.'

'Wonderboy is mine. My father gave him to me.'

'The Cobbler is mine.'

They looked at each other gravely for a moment and then Paul grinned and said: 'I'm not supposed to tell you, but the Captain's in the feed shed. He's hiding.'

Callie still could not see her mother, but she went to the feed shed door alone, instead of going out to look for Anna in the car. Jean said that she was too dependent, and hinted that her mother spoiled her, although she called it 'sheltered'. So this she would do by herself, without help.

When she opened the door and shut it quickly behind her, because two curious women were peering after her, she said: 'Oh,' and stopped with her back against the door. Anna was sitting on a broad wooden feed bin, swinging her legs girlishly as she was not supposed to do, and talking to the Captain. She told Callie at once, seeing her face, which she had screwed up on to tenterhooks before she came in, that Wonderboy was safe.

'Jean will be angry,' was Callie's first reaction, without thinking.

'Oh no. Do you think she wanted the horse destroyed just for the fun of it?'

'I don't know.' Callie rubbed her hands across her eyes. 'I don't know why I said that. I hadn't thought of it before.'

'Forget it now.' Anna held out her hand. 'Come on. I know what you've been through.' The uncertainty, the guilt of power over life and death wrongly used. The night visions of the proud bold horse crumpled in the straw with his shining chocolate coat dulled and his eye glazing over. The galloping dreams of John to torture her with the reproach: Would you destroy this last part of me?

'It's over now. Everything is all right. Come on. Come over here and thank the Captain.'

They shook hands, and Callie, still a little shocked with relief, gravely considered the face of the man whose step and voice and smell would become Wonderboy's creed, as her father's and then hers had been. A door opened under the cobwebbed rafters at the far end of the barn where the hay and the chaff cutter were, and Mrs Berry in a flutter of scarves and stoles came in by what she had appropriated as her private entrance, stopping at the poultry stacks for a handful of maize.

'I knew it,' said the Captain. 'Come on, let's go and settle this up at the house.'

At the door, he said: 'Have to make a dash for it.' Pulling his coat collar up over the back of his head as if it was raining, he dashed under the archway and round through the cover of a bedraggled shrubbery to the front of the house, with Anna and Callie after him like hounds.

'I've stacked them,' Tiny said. 'I've made all neat. But that's as far as I will go. Don't anybody ask me to read them, for the pony would be dead of old age long before I finished.'

'I haven't asked you to read them.' The Captain looked lugubriously at the piles of letters on a card table in the small front room which was his office. 'I'll do it when I get time.'

'Let me put them in the boiler. Come on, love.'

Tiny made a lunge at the table, and the Captain said: 'No!' fiercely, because he had battled for years against being called Love, especially in front of strangers. 'One of them is probably the perfect home for Mickey. It wouldn't be fair to give him away until I've read them all.'

'Then you'll need a secretary. I've just made his tea,' Tiny said to Anna, neither graciously nor ungraciously. 'Will you take a cup?'

'Thank you.' When Tiny had gone out, and the Captain sat down behind his desk and began to push papers and ledgers about to find what he needed, Anna sat opposite him and said diffidently, glancing first at Callie and then at her thin hands, but not at all at the Captain: 'If you'd like it, I'd be glad to try and help. I think I can type and take shorthand well enough to do the answers. At least I used to be able to. I'm –'

She stopped herself before she could say: 'I'm a bit rusty.' Defeated phrase. Phrase of useless, ill-trained women who were a drag on their family if they were not employed, and a drag on their employers if they were. Feeble, useless widows who had not planned for widowhood.

'I'm sure I could do it,' she said.

Driving up the hill to the Farm on Monday, with the car losing on the bends what little heart it ever had, Anna Sheppard was not as happy as she had been driving home on Saturday.

She had expected to please her daughter-in-law by finding work so soon; but Jean's first question had been: 'What's he going to pay you?' and it was only then that Anna realized that in the excitement of getting her first job for twenty years, she had forgotten why she needed it.

She stood looking at Jean blankly, turning her toes in, as she did when she was taken aback. 'I think I'm doing it for nothing.'

Jean peered at her to see if it was a joke, and Anna said quickly: 'The place is run mostly on charity, you see. Callie's going to pay two shillings a week for Wonderboy, just to make her feel he's still hers, but most of the horses have no one paying for them. If it wasn't for the Farm, they –'

Jean was not interested in the hazards of a beast of burden. 'You can't afford to work for nothing,' she said, and left the words: *and let Peter support you* to impose themselves soundlessly between them.

'I know,' Anna laughed nervously. 'Of course I know. It was all settled so quickly, and the man who runs the Farm – he's no more businesslike than I am. He's sure of his work, but at the same time a little lost, like a person who knows where he's going, but needs someone to read the map.'

'Anna,' said Jean unmollified, 'you'll have to go back and tell him that he's either got to pay you a standard wage, or find himself another victim.'

'It won't be easy.' You tell him, Anna was going to say, but that would not be fair on the Captain. 'I'll try it, if you want.'

'It's not what *I* want. It's for you and Callie. Don't pull down your face, Anna. I'm only trying to help you.'

'You're a dear,' Anna squeezed her arm, and pretended not to notice that she stiffened slightly away. Jean had a complex about any kind of caress. Anna had discovered this when Peter came in with his hair on end and shouted that they were going to be married, and Anna had come running down the stairs and across the floor, spontaneously to kiss her.

Mustn't sulk. Mustn't quarrel. Don't be mean to Jean. Here we are. Me and Callie. Left without a bean. The doggerel jogged in her head as she drove up the serpentine hill to the Farm, rehearsing and rejecting twenty different ways to ask the Captain for money.

When she finally came out with it, in the stable where she

had run him to earth, putting a bran poultice on Dolly's infected foot, he was as embarrassed as she was.

Squatting in the straw, keeping his head down, he said: 'You didn't think I expected you to –'

'Well, yes, I –'

'But then, why did you –'

'It was only when I –'

He tied the hot wet bran bag round the top of Dolly's hoof, and stood up and smiled at Anna, crinkling the corner of the eye that was not stretched by the scar. On the way back to the house, she boldly suggested half of what Jean had told her to demand, the Captain raised it by another quarter, and everyone was happy. Including Jean, because Anna tacked on the missing quarter when she reported the deal at home.

There were hundreds of letters to be read and sorted and answered. Some of them were heartbreaking, some were infuriating, more than half were quite impossible, if you were seeking a good home for an animal, rather than gratifying the whim of a human. Anna was free to answer the impossible chaff in her own way, and the others were winnowed out into a smaller pile from which the Captain would select the fate of the black and white Shetland pony.

It was a long job for anyone, and it took Anna longer, not only because her typing was as rusty as she had feared and because she spent too much sympathy on the kind of letters she and Callie might have written, but because people kept coming in and talking to her.

In spite of Tiny Jones' efforts to keep the Captain on a higher plane from everyone but herself, his office, which had a door at each end, was treated as the passage it might once have been by anyone travelling from front to back at that side of the house.

Paul often came in on the way to his room at the top of the back stairs. In Anna's experience, boys did not go up to their rooms as often as this during the day, especially when they had as few clothes as Paul. But he always lingered going through, for her to look up and say something, so that he could talk.

He told her, in snatches, that his father had died when he was a baby and his mother two years ago, since when he had been

60

on his own. He was vague about the date of his mother's death, and how he had lived immediately after. Too big a shock, Anna thought. He had to wipe it from his memory.

It had obviously hurt him badly. Beyond his fierce love for the pony, and the strange understanding between them, he was destitute of care and affection. Tiny threw some at him in her rough, unsubtle way, and boiled the life out of his clothes as diligently as Slugger's, and Anna was glad to offer him the warmth that Peter had politely fended off at Paul's age.

Dora was different. She lounged inquisitively in and out with her hands in her pockets, because she wanted to get a look at the letters, not because she needed mothering. She had had too much of that. As Anna gradually became an accepted member of the Farm, typing away at her card table, Dora told her why she had got away so young.

'It was the horses. Yes, that. I'd always wanted to work somewhere like this. But it was just having to get away.' She dropped a paperweight and bent to pick it up. When she talked, she leaned on furniture and fiddled with things, like a small boy. 'At home, they watched me. They didn't like what they saw, but they watched me. They all watch each other like guinea pigs, and discuss what they do and how they feel and whether they mean exactly what they say, and if not, what's the truth? When I was a child and I was naughty, they didn't just smack me and forget it. We'd have long serious talks, rationalizing, analysing what I'd done and why I'd done it. Moral responsibility. Mother would plug that into me in a precise, patient voice, and then try to make me explain it back to her. I never could, so I decided long ago to get away as soon as I could leave school.'

'Why did they let you?' Anna reached forward to rescue some letters, as Dora leaned her hip against the table.

'Glad to get me out of the way, I suppose. They've got dozens of friends who come in bubble cars and gas their kind of stuff. I was always like a footstool under the table.' Dora chewed the skin round a nail. 'Do you mind me telling you this? There's no one else to discuss it with. Mrs Catchpole would fold her hands and say: Mothers are mothers the world over, without really listening. Tiny – she just might understand, but she's usually making so much noise she can't hear you. The Captain is centuries too old –'

'So am I then.' Anna smiled.

'Honest? How old are you?'

When Anna told her, she said casually: 'Well, never mind,' and went on: 'And Paul is too young. With him, it's either got to be about horses or about himself.'

'He's older than you.'

'But boys stay conceited longer. Children say I all the time, and have long conversations about *my* favourite colour, what *I* like to eat, without listening to each other. The girls grow out of it before the boys. Haven't you noticed?'

She stood up straight and rubbed at the place on her slacks where the edge of the table had dug in. If she went now, Anna would be able to finish two dozen more letters before she went home. But she never pushed Dora or Paul out when they wanted to talk, in case they did not come back. She was proud of their confidence and refreshed by the current of outdoors and youth that moved in with them to the cramped, low-ceilinged room. She had lived with John and Callie long enough to accept the faint smell of stables that came with it.

'My daughter is very jealous of you,' she said, as Dora went to the door.

'So would I have been at her age. I wanted to be with horses so badly for so long, it was like a disease. But Callie will never be strong enough for a job like this.'

'Why not?'

'Sickly. Besides,' continued Dora with the same bluntness, 'you'd never let her. That's the only snag about having a proper mother.'

The Captain was not in his office very much. It seemed as if everyone used it but him. Slugger Jones kept some plants in there that needed a north light, and Mrs Berry, violet scented, came in to write cheques for Evrémonde, and letters of protest on the Farm's stationery. She wrote to the Prime Minister inquiring why he did not shoot clay pigeons instead of his feathered friends, and she wrote to Buckingham Palace about the Queen riding in a headscarf, and about a Lifeguardsman she had seen in the Park with a twisted curb-chain.

Tiny, passing through with a pile of harsh towels under her square chin, or to check that Anna was not setting fire to the waste-paper basket, told her that the Captain spent too much time in the stables.

'It's horses, horses, all day long with him,' she said, standing square as a monolith in a felt skirt that was as broad as long, with woollen knee socks on the sturdy legs below it. 'What is the sense of him hiring all those old men and children and then going out and doing half their work for them? Not that they don't need watching. My Jones is the only one who knows what he's doing.'

'He's wonderful with the horses. I've watched him,' Anna lied.

'Ah, he is.' Tiny sat down like the Lincoln memorial, massive, at rest. 'He was training to be a jockey once, you know, till he left the turf for the ring. Good little fighter he was too. Flyweight. Dead on scale. Never had to diet him.' Her smile of pride in the things she loved, like Slugger, and her small hedge-row babies, and the old boxing years, was very broad and soft.

'Those were the days though,' she mused, as Anna was silent, sneaking her eyes back to work. 'They'd not let me inside the ropes – they think it's a man's world, which is a delusion common to many walks of life – but I'd be at his corner, passing up the sponges and swabs and telling him what he had to do.'

'How did you know?' Anna stopped trying to read a letter from a woman who wanted a pony to pull her old mother in a basket chair.

'I was in the game myself, you see.' Tiny set her big mouth tight and stern below the shadow of moustache. 'Wrestling. That was my line.' She put her hands on her broad knees and looked at Anna speculatively. 'I could throw you now with one arm behind my back if I had a mind. I throw my Jones sometimes, just to keep my hand in. He doesn't relish it, so I take him unawares, when there's grass or a carpet under-foot.'

When the Captain came in to work at his desk, or look through some of the letters, he seldom stayed very long. He seemed confined in the narrow room. Even on chill days, when he flung open a window and set Anna's flesh rising, he would begin after a while to pass his hand restlessly over his face, dabbing at the broad forehead, massaging the narrow jaw. 'Stuffy in here.' And he would soon go out of doors.

The window opposite his desk looked out on to a paddock at the side of the house. The Weaver, the bay Police horse who rocked from foot to foot endlessly with his head still and his neck swaying like a hypnotized chicken, liked to stand and weave at the fence of this field. From a neurotic mare who used to be in the next box, he had picked up the habit of cribbing: setting his top teeth on the edge of the manger or the top of the door, arching his neck and taking in a great noisy gulp of air like an old man after a good lunch.

When he got tired of weaving in the field, he would begin to crib on the top rail of the fence outside the window, and you could swear he did it to annoy. With vacant eye, legs braced in the muddy patch he had trodden, he would set his neck against the hold of his long curved teeth, and you could actually see the air go down and hear the disgusting noise it made, even with the window shut.

With a muffled roar, the Captain would spring from his chair and rush out of the house to drive the bay horse away from the fence. The Weaver would wait until things had quieted down and the Captain was back in his office. Then he would be back at the fence, licking the battered rail for a while before he took hold again, set his neck, and – 'Arr-a-a-a –'. Out would rush the Captain, brandishing the ash plant he kept by the side door.

Once when Tiny was in the room and he rushed out like that, she said: 'You'd swear that animal does it on purpose. Miles of fence to belch on, but it has to be this one, with his eye on the boss to keep him hopping. He never sits long at anything, doesn't the Captain. Won't even stay in bed some nights. I'll hear him pacing, or the back door will slam shut and my Jones shoot up in bed like a ghost and cry: "They've got us!" but it will be the Captain going out for a prowl.'

'He ought to be married,' Anna said.

Tiny laughed, down in her deep chest. 'He is. Married to those horses. Where do you think he goes at night? Not that he hasn't had his chances. I could tell you some things. Photo in his room.' She jerked her head sideways and up, her lips compressed. 'I say no more.'

'It's probably his sister,' Anna started to say, but Slugger put his punchball of a head round the door and said to the opposite wall: 'I'm looking for her to make my dinner.'

Chapter Seven

After Wonderboy had been fetched in the Farm's horse-box and respectfully installed with his name in white letters over the door, Callie suffered school like an allergy, and yearned towards the Farm like dune grass leaning in the sea wind.

She could hardly bear her mother to be there every day, and Anna often had to make a second trip back after school, so that Callie could worship at the shrine of the dark dapple-brown horse, and savour his sweet hay breath, and hazard tall tales of his past triumphs to anyone who would stop to listen.

Surprisingly, it was often Ronnie Stryker who stopped in his panther stride to listen. Although he was a cynic with no time for kids, his very cynicism showed her to him as pathetic, because he had been so much less juvenile at her age. Also he was lazy, and easily distracted from work.

Anna would not be going to the Farm much longer. The letters were nearly done, and she would have to find another job. Jean had threatened to get her into the Town Hall typing pool, which was a brisk incentive to find something else. It was Callie who suggested that she might offer to come in one evening a week to help with the Captain's regular letters and bills. 'If it's not too much for you as well as a job,' she said, with the fear always in the back of her mind that her mother would sicken and die. 'But it would keep us in touch.'

When Anna ventured it, the Captain said the same thing. 'I'll be glad not to lose touch with you both,' he said.

The Animal Man wanted to do another television show, since the first had been so popular, but the Captain refused, to Ronnie's disgust ('Next time I was going to have me guitar along'), and the Farm relaxed once more into obscurity as the plum blossom blew away before the warming winds that lapped along the top of the hills.

After some argument, with the five best letters passed among all the staff and no one agreeing, Mickey was awarded to a family of five children on a fruit farm. The newspapers, who had helped to work up the hue and cry over the pony, had lost interest long ago and did not even report who finally got him. Any news over two weeks old was ancient history, and so the Shetland left unsung, except by his stable mate, shrilly, her tiny hoofs tattooing the door, and by the five enraptured faces in the back window of the car which towed Mickey away in a home-made trailer.

After the first rush of curious visitors, the summer settled down into its usual pattern of weekday stragglers and bunches on a fine Sunday. The usual questions were asked and willingly answered, for there was no one at the stable who was not glad to talk about the horses. Even Ronnie, who did not like them as much as he had expected after a childhood orchestrated by gun-shots and galloping hoofs, enjoyed parading himself as their master.

The usual brash children were pulled down off the doors, and called in from the fences where they were poised for a flying leap on to some venerable grazing spine. The usual perennial tales were told about each horse. How the brown mare, inevitably nicknamed Pussycat, had been on her way to London to see the Queen. How Flame, the gaunt old thoroughbred, had been con-demned to end her racing days in a shoddy riding stable, where she was deliberately starved so that oafs and beginners could ride her. How Fanny with the empty shrivelled eye socket had lost the eye to the flailing stick of a drunken gipsy. How Mrs Berry, the ugly roan, would eat your hat or your gloves or the buttons off your coat if he got the chance. 'If we were to X-ray him,' it was said, 'we'd find enough to start a lost property office.'

Round some of the oldest inhabitants, there had grown up over the years legends whose truth and origin no one but Uncle knew. And Uncle was glad to invent for effect where nobody could check.

'This here is the oldest horse you ever will see,' he would say, giving the pit pony his calloused palm. Charley could not mumble at you softly with a warm rubbery muzzle. His teeth

67

were so long and so loose in his gums that they stuck out below his mouth like a rabbit. He would grate them gently on Uncle's hand, blinking his scant and faded eyelashes as Uncle told the visitors that he was forty.

He was more likely thirty, but he had been through so many hands since he came up to the surface that no one knew his age, not even which pit he came from. Uncle billed him as 'the oldest horse that ever lived', but even if he were forty, he was a youngster compared to such veterans as the American racehorse Old Romp, who died at fifty-two, and the famous draught-horse Old Billy, who was claimed by the greybeard who bred him to be over sixty when he died in eighteen-twenty-one.

But the Girl Guides and the schoolteacher with the jostling, clowning class, and the families on a day out were quite satisfied, and the women said to each other: 'Fancy,' and sucked their teeth and said: 'A-a-ah,' in a soppy way. The brisker, brighter ones did not query sagging old Charley's claim to fame, since they were too busy offering the worn-out fallacy: 'But I thought all pit ponies were blind!'

A surprise visitor one Saturday morning was Chrissy in a precocious flowered hat and a pale blue suit which did nothing for her bolster shape. Paul was out at the Dutch barn checking a delivery of straw, and he recognized the big shiny car and the chauffeur who drove it in.

There was a notice by the main gate asking people to leave their cars on the grass at the side of the road. But Chrissy had herself brought into the driveway, and probably would have driven right through the grey stone archway into the stableyard if it had been wide enough for the opulent fat car.

She had seen the television show, and ever since had been 'begging and begging' her father to let her come over and see darling Cobby.

'I always though you only took him to spite me, not to keep him. I couldn't believe it when I turned on the set and there he was. And you too. Jeekers – you did look funny! Were you made up?'

'No.' Paul made for the archway with his head down, and she followed him.

'Don't be sulky, Paul. I thought you'd be glad to see me. I'm awfully glad to see you, really I am.' She gushed, which was worse than her usual sullen spite. But there were quite a few people about for an audience, and to Paul's disgust, she took his arm and clung to him, chattering sweetly up into his face as they crossed the yard.

He brushed her off like a fly. 'Cut it out, Chrissy. What's the matter with you?'

She pinched him in the tender flesh of the upper arm, the simper still sugaring her cold pudding face.

He took her to Cobby's stable, and was glad to see that the pony laid back the keen crescents of his ears and took a nip at her.

'He's still as mean as ever, I see.' Chrissy stepped back and eyed the pony, with her hands clasped behind her.

'If you'd held out your hand for him to smell, instead of throwing it up to his nose, he wouldn't have nipped,' Paul said. 'You've been around horses long enough to know that.'

'Not this kind of horse,' Chrissy said. 'The one I have now is an angel. She lets me do anyfing wiv her.' She pouted, slipping into baby-talk.

'Must be drugged,' said Paul, and the fat child scowled at Cobby and said: 'He's always been tricky. That Mason girl should have told us when we bought him. Unless it was you that made him mean. After what you did to him at the end, we shouldn't be surprised at anything, Daddy says.'

'After what I –' Had she actually worked herself round to believing her own lie? Paul clenched his hands. If the yard had not been full of people, he might have grabbed her neck and shaken her until her eyes rolled like marbles.

'He's much too fat anyway,' she said smugly, 'and his mane's all grown in ragged. He looks awful. Why ever did you keep him?'

Paul was disgusted, but he was not going to leave her alone with the Cobbler. She could not hit him here, but a poisoned lump of sugar would be right in her line. 'Why did you come all the way over here if you'd rather he were dead?' he asked.

'*I* wasn't the one who wanted him put down.' She opened her pale eyes as wide as they would go. 'I wanted to keep him and be good to him. It was you who said he was no use any more. Don't you remember?'

Paul stared at her, baffled; but as Chrissy began to smarm and coo over the Cobbler, he saw that Dora had come up behind him, and this was for her benefit.

'Telling the Animal Man he could jump six feet! Wasn't that a scream? Oh, I could have died.' Chrissy giggled, hand to mouth. She mimicked what Paul had said: 'He'd never jump really big for anyone but me,' smirking, wriggling her lumpy hips.

'This is the girl who used to own the Cobbler,' Paul mumbled, and Dora asked brightly: 'The one you said rode like a sack of wet sawdust?'

Chrissy made a face like the hunchback playing gargoyle among the pinnacles of Notre Dame. 'I came third last week at Hillsborough, so yah.' The childishness did not go with the precocious petalled hat.

'Must be a foolproof pony you've got.' The Captain called from across the yard and Paul had to leave Chrissy with Dora. He would have to tell her afterwards that whatever the little rat told her, it was a lie.

Paul went off with the Captain on an ambulance call to a horse that had got into wire, and he did not see Dora until the next morning.

Since Ronnie Stryker was the only one who lived away from the Farm, the others usually took his Sunday shifts for him, but once in a while the Captain made him come up from the village on a Sunday for the good of his soul, cheap fodder or no cheap fodder.

'My Uncle won't like this. Not one little bit he won't.' Ronnie was grumbling back and forth between the stables and the tap, sloshing water on his pointed boots, cursing at the horses as if they and not the Captain had ordered him to work.

'He's a very religious man, is my uncle,' he told Dora, who was filling the buckets for him and Paul to carry, although Ronnie had wasted ten minutes arguing that it was his turn to fill and hers to carry. 'No servile work on a Sunday, he says, and he won't let Auntie as much as shake out a cloth. Servile work, that's what this is, and he is dead against it.'

'Perhaps he will say that you can't work here any more,' Dora said hopefully.

''Tis my fervent prayer that he may.' Ronnie lurched off, leaning far enough over to soak her tattered gym shoes.

Later when the work was finished, they were down at the end of the low raftered barn, stacking away the forks and shovels and wheelbarrows.

'If a horse wasn't so dumb, you could house train it like a dog,' Ronnie said. 'Then we should all die happy.' He lit a cigarette, for he had heard the Captain's car start up and knew that he had gone to church. He flicked the match away, and Paul said: 'There goes twenty tons of hay.'

'Save forking it, if so.' Ronnie winked and held out the packet of cigarettes. 'No? You're astonishing virtuous since you been here, Curly.'

'Don't call me that.'

'Quite a change, I might say.'

'From what?' Paul did not know how much Ronnie knew, for he was coward enough to stop the innuendoes if he was challenged.

'Oh – I don't know.' Ronnie shrugged his weedy shoulders under a bright green shirt which tied at the neck with a red plastic cord. 'Just talking.' He flicked cigarette ash on to the wooden floor, strewn with chaff and dusty hay seeds, and said very casually: 'Saw one of your old pals last night.'

'Who?'

'The Hyena. Old laughing jackal himself. At the Palais. That's his beat now, Saturdays, if you want to renew acquaintance.'

'I never met him.'

'Funny thing. He asked after you. Quite touching really. The Hyena isn't usually that concerned about anyone.'

'The Hyena?' asked Dora, and Paul wished that she would shut up, for Ronnie was ambling towards the door, and might have let it go at that. 'Who's he?'

'One of the boys.' Ronnie stopped and turned. 'Very powerful man in his own district. Ask anyone.' He jerked his head towards Paul.

'He doesn't know him.' Dora did not doubt people unless they shoved the lie under her nose labelled Lie, don't believe me. 'Why is he called the Hyena?'

'Because he can do this terrible laugh, see?' Ronnie suddenly pounced towards her, hands curved into claws, letting out a blood-curdling cackle like the sound track in an old horror film. Dora stepped back against a bale of hay and sat on it. 'When you hear that late some night under the railway arches, you know you've had it. That right, Curly? Oh, beg pardon. I forgot. You don't know him. Quite right. Quite right. Fine young chap like you, you want to stay out of trouble.' He sucked back his diaphragm to tuck the lurid shirt into his high waistband, whipped out a comb whose passage made scant impression on his bush of hair, scraped his feet backwards two or three times like a runner, cried: 'I'm off!' and sauntered whistling out of the barn.

'But you have already been in trouble, haven't you?' Dora did not ask it. She stated it candidly.

'Who says?'

'That horrid girl who came to see Cobby yesterday. She told me you'd been in Borstal.'

'It's a lie. She'd say anything to make trouble. And you believed her.'

'I'm afraid I did.' She saw his angry face, the blue eyes hard, the boyish mouth twisted into a scowl. 'Shouldn't I have?'

'It makes you as bad as her.'

'No, because she thinks it's shameful. I don't.'

'What else did she tell you?'

'That you hit Cobby over the eye with a whip. I didn't believe *that*, of course. But the way she told it, shifting her eyes from side to side and not looking at me – she wouldn't even look at the Cobbler – I thought perhaps it hadn't been an accident at all, but she had done it.'

Paul did not say anything.

'She did, didn't she?'

'Oh well.' Paul slumped down beside her on the bale of hay, not looking at her. He put a stalk in his mouth and bit off the dried clover head savagely. 'So she had to rat on me. Just when I'd got a new start. Just when I could be anything I wanted,

72

with no one blaming me, watching me, trying to set me – yes, all right, I was in Borstal. So what?'

'So nothing.' Dora leaned back against the bales behind her and kicked up her feet. 'I don't care.'

'I knew that little beast didn't come here to see the Cobbler,' Paul went on. 'She never liked him, because she wasn't good enough for him. She came here just to put a knife in my back.'

'But why?'

'Because I know about her. She hit Cobby on purpose. She blinded him. It was the vet who said it must have been an accident. No one knew the truth but her and me.'

'It was pretty nice of you not to tell on her. She didn't deserve loyalty.'

'No.' Paul frowned. 'I wasn't being loyal. I'm not like that. I just – I don't know – I didn't want to tell. Because I could blackmail her into getting the Cobbler for me.'

'You've just thought of that,' Dora guessed.

'They wouldn't have believed me anyway. They thought I was a liar.'

'Well you are,' Dora said. 'Why?'

'Search me. I used to lie as a child. Not to hurt people, I don't think, but to get myself out of trouble. There was always plenty of that. I had no father. He died. He died when I was a baby, and I was sort of dragged up. Mother didn't have a chance. She wasn't the type to manage a child.'

'What was she like?'

'Soft,' he said after a moment. 'Soft, you know, and gentle. Like – like Callie's mother.'

Mum, dressed for going out with some man or other – the latest in the procession of fake uncles – in the tight pillowcase of black satin, with her legs running straight down into her shoes. She with her harsh dyed hair like sea grass, bleached so many times it would not take the colour properly. Me in our big lopsided bed, watching her with my chin and paws over the blanket like a mouse, scared to death to be left alone, but too scared to beg her not to go. Or too proud?

'It's hard for a woman to be a mother and father both,' Dora said in a grave, adult voice, to show that she was paying attention.

'I can't have been much more than two when my father was killed. There was an accident at the steel works. Mother told me about it years afterwards, and how she screamed and bit the cushions when they came and told her.'

Her story that was, and she stuck to it all through. Even to me, she never let on that Dad walked out on her because he couldn't stand it. And afraid I'd be like her, I suppose, for how could a man not want to see his son – just once, say – out of curiosity? Gran said he would, that night she let on he wasn't dead, and kept looking over her shoulder for fear a living ghost would haunt her. Well, I'm still waiting, Dad, but now I don't need you.

'So then of course she had to work and I was partly with her in the little house we had along the canal, but mostly with Gran and the old man out the other side of town. That was all right. The old man was a horse dealer. I learned to ride everything, handle everything. He knew all the tricks. Matching up the horse's coat with shoe polish to hide the scars and galls, banging one leg with a hammer if the other was lame, to make the pair go sound. I remember one we had that was broken winded. When I had to show it off, the old man started up the power saw to drown the noise it made.'

Paul chuckled, and Dora said: 'Didn't you think he was cruel?'

'I do now. I didn't then. Not at first. He had all the say. You didn't question him. He was all I had for a father, and Mother didn't – well, she didn't know what went on, because she wasn't there, except when she'd get lonely for me and fetch me back to town.'

She'd come on the bus. No warning. Suddenly the fancy trodden-over shoes and the green coat with the glitter buttons that shrieked in the country. 'Paul, my Paulie, my darling boy!' Unless I'd seen her coming and hid in the hay loft. That time she came drunk, and Gran didn't want to let me go. 'Why don't you get an axe and split the boy in two?' the old man said, watching them at it. 'Then you'll both be satisfied.' He didn't care either way. Gran was the only one.

'Gran didn't like that. She wanted me to stay. My grandmother – she was the one who should have had charge of the

horses really, but she knew better than to interfere. She was
dark, like a gipsy, and she had a fiddle. She played it for me.
Wild old songs that you couldn't put words to, like the voice of
the wind. Once in a while when the old man went to town, she'd
sneak out and play it to the horses. You think that's funny?'
He scanned Dora's amiable expression aggressively. 'It wasn't.
"You can see in their eyes what they hear in the music," she said.
When I was old enough, she began to tell me secret things
about talking to animals. Feelings she'd caught from them. De-
sires. Thoughts she understood. I believed her then, and I still
do in a way, though I know it only works with certain ones.'

'Like Cobby.'

'Yes. Like Cobby. There was a horse came in one day that
the old man picked up at a sale. A little fine grey with an Arab
head. Much too good for our place, but he was wild and scary
and the word had got round that he was mean. He wasn't. Just
nervous. He and I knew each other right away. We – well, we
talked, Gran would say. I could do anything with him, but he
was funny with anyone else, so I asked the old man to give him
to me. Pathetic, the ideas kids get. He wanted to price Cloud
right up, because of his looks, so he yoked him to a tree trunk
that was much too heavy, and lashed him to break his spirit
trying to pull it. I came home from school and found him at it,
and I got the whip away and hit the old man with it, and after
that he told Gran I couldn't stay there any more, so Mother
took me away.'

*Must have been a good two weeks before she stopped yelling
at me. It was when Gran sent the picture of Cloud she'd taken,
and Mum got the envelope open and tore it up. She shut up
then. She'd won. Sick, blind rage. What did I do? Coming out
of it was like fighting up out of heavy sleep. Me on the floor,
with my eye against the hole in the carpet where the castor had
stood so long without a wheel. She over by the window scared,
with the back of her hand in her mouth and all over lipstick –
cyclamen it was those days – and the curtain behind her half
off its rod.*

'I didn't like the school in town. I left as soon as I could.'

'So did I,' Dora said. 'They lecture you about staying on, but
I'll never regret it. Freedom and a job. That's living.'

'Of a kind.' Paul looked carefully at her honest, uncomplicated face. If life were only that simple. Perhaps it was, if you were Dora. 'Mother was at the box factory then. She got me in as a packer. I hated the job and the pay was nothing and I knew I was a drag on her, so I ran away.'

Away, away from the sour smells in the gutters and the mean little house that was grey all over, flint, slates and the overall veil of dirt. Away from her tongue and the dry hairs in her brush and the beer bottles and the cold loneliness at night. Worse when she was at home or when she went out? She was mostly out. Her friends were no longer Uncle, pretending to like me. Uncle Gilbert, who brought the little drum, and kicked me when she was out of the room. Now I stared at them and hated. And they stared back and hated me.

'I ran to my grandmother, and she wasn't there any more. The stable was a garage and the paddock full of old broken-up cars. After the old man died, she'd sold up and gone to live with his sister. I found her, but she'd gone queer in the head, a little. She couldn't catch on. They both thought I'd just come for a visit, so I waited till after dinner and then got going. I couldn't find work, so I stole a bit of food here and there, and after a few days I went home.'

'Your mother must have been mad with worry.' Dora was not shocked, but any woman like Callie's mother would have been half out of her mind.

The door locked against me. The blind, shut dirty windows. I knew you were there inside. Don't ever think I didn't. Why do you think I stood there trying to bang the door down, with half the women down the street out to stare?

'She was dead,' Paul said shortly, and stood up. 'That's all. She'd been – been hit by a car and died in the hospital. The Police told me.'

He turned round to face Dora, twisting his mouth together to keep it firm, and Dora jumped up and put her arm round him, her eyes full of tears, and cried: 'Oh, Paul – how terrible for you!'

'Just one of those things.' He moved away from her strong, friendly arm, irked by the sincerity of her pity. You lied to people because you wanted them to believe you, and then resented it when they did. 'I got by. Stealing food got so easy, I was careless and got myself nabbed. Lovely old woman in a bakery. Instead of turning me in, she gave me to the Youth Officer, and he took me in his house and fed me, and got me a job in the brewery after a bit, when he found I hadn't anybody.'

I told you Michael, not to go looking for her. But you had this thing about mothers. She'd got to know where I was, and that I was all right. Did you think she'd care? I'd give anything to know just what she'd said to you when you came back looking battered, and flung at me in a casual way I could stay on.

'The brewery was all right. I wasn't allowed in the stables, but I could sneak in when the stud groom was off and inhale a little horse smell to cancel out the hops. Michael was all right too, poor guy. We had to call him Michael, to show no barriers. Missionary type. He was reforming half a dozen boys who'd been in trouble. Kindness. Understanding. Healthy activities. The lot. They were building a boat in a shed back of his house. How his wife stood it I don't know, but she fed them like lords and would have mothered them too, but they wouldn't go that far. They'd go along with Michael because it tickled their fancy to get so much attention, and there was the food and the billiard table and a club room with coke and a good record player, but none of them had any idea of going straight.'

'One of them was Ronnie Stryker,' Dora hazarded.

'No, but I did see him around now and then. He runs on the outside of that gang. He hasn't guts enough to be mixed right in with them, but he spies around and knows what's going on. Listen Dora.' He crossed his arms and frowned at her. 'I wasn't going to tell anyone this. I'll kill you if you ever say a word. But you know about Borstal, so you may as well know who put me there.'

'Not Michael?' Dora was in this now up to the neck, eyes shining, loving it.

'One of his pets. Big vicious boy who could soap poor old Michael right up the wall. Skipper of the boat, he was going to be, if it ever got launched. Pride of the Youth Club, but he'd have had a record as long as your arm if he'd been caught only half of the time.'

'The Hyena,' Dora breathed, her small boyish figure tense, fists clenched at the side of the red slacks.

Paul nodded, recapturing in her excitement the old glamour of the Hyena and his lot who were so swaggering sure of their power, who used the good and guileless Michael so casually, who called Paul Curlybaby, because he looked more innocent than his life had made him.

'I was like a sort of mascot to them. Not that much younger, but I didn't mind them calling me Curly and teasing me, because I thought they had all the answers, and I was flattered – dumb little jerk I was – to be in with them. They were going to do a cigarette warehouse, down by the river. It would be their biggest yet, and the Hyena planned it all in the boat shed when poor old Michael was out scouting for delinquents. Working in the Field, he called it. My ears were too big to keep me out of it, and they needed me anyway, for there had to be an extra lookout, in case of the Police boat on the river. I suppose *you* –' he thrust out his chin at Dora – 'think I ought to have told Michael what was going on.'

'Why do you keep accusing me of being smug?' Dora sat down again and put her chin on her knees, hugging them. 'Go on. It's thrilling. I can see why you went in with the Hyena. That's the way boys go wrong. Hero worship. They get corrupted by someone they admire.'

'Wise old girl, aren't you? But you could be right. Our Mascot. I'd never been anything like that to anyone. I felt like a stray puppy who's found somewhere to belong. I thought I could trust them. I was in with them, and they'd stick by me. How simple can you get? The scare was raised at the other end of the warehouse and they all got away and left me standing on the river steps like the boy on the burning deck, except that I was up to the ankles in water.'

'So you were caught.' Dora sighed. It was a logical ending to the story.

'The others had got back to the shed and were working like mad on the boat. Swore they'd been there all evening, and Michael backed them up, although he'd only just come home, because he thought he'd done such a good job on them, they couldn't possibly be in trouble. And the Hyena got them all to

78

swear that I had told them about the raid and the gang I was planning it with, but they were too noble to say who.'

'I hate them,' Dora said placidly. 'I hope you denounced them in Court.'

'I was dumb in Court. The magistrate asked me if I'd lost my tongue, so I stuck it out at him.'

Who could talk, with Mum sitting there in the lavender outfit, looking worse than I remembered? But still that wild flick of hope that she'd come to help me. Standing up with her hands on that great black plastic bag like a coal bin: 'I've done my best, but I can't do anything with him.' The righteous bit. 'He's been bad all his life. Never anything but worry to me. No sir. I'm sorry. I'm just a widow woman with my living to make.' The humble bit. 'I couldn't manage him now.'

'I went to Borstal, and the Hyena and his lot went on building that crazy boat. They sent me a Christmas card with a picture Michael had taken of them rigging it. "Nice Day for a Sail."'

'I hope it sank.'

'Probably would too, the way that lot work. They'd drill a hole in the bottom just to spite old Michael. Anyone who did anything for them – they'd as soon cut his throat as look at him. They'd have cut mine, if I'd ever told. Still would, I guess, but I'll cut theirs first. The Hyena and I – we'll meet one of these days, and he'll find out that Curlybaby don't forget.'

Getting out of Borstal, with the vague idea of finding the Hyena and beating him up. Feeling almost as badly about Mum, but where else to go? Strange face at the door, even worse than hers. Thin woman in curlers, like a witch, with a moulting broomstick in her hand. 'Oh no, there's no one of that name here.' But she was a local. She knew what I'd done and where I'd been. Mr Dreyer pretending not to be a warden: 'Could you give me my cousin's new address?' Quite friendly and casual. 'We're respectable folk here!' After she'd slammed the door in his face, I thought she'd take off up the chimney on that broomstick.

'And if you ever tell what I've told you,' Paul leaned over and thrust his face close to Dora's, 'I'll cut yours too.'

Dora gulped and pitched backwards. His boyish face was so

harsh and violent, she almost believed him. 'Suppose Ronnie tells?'

'I think he's too yellow. He knows I'd get him. Like I'll get you if you tell anyone, and especially the Captain, about Borstal and that.'

Dora licked her finger and went through the schoolgirl throat routine with a solemn face. 'Trust me.'

Chapter Eight

It did not need the vet to diagnose that Cobby's right eye was beginning to fail. Paul knew him so well that he could tell at once.

In six months, the pony had adapted himself cleverly to his blind left eye. He was sure-footed and no longer carried his head slightly on one side, peering. There were no saddles at the Farm, since the old horses were there to rest, not work; but Cobby was only nine and bouncing fit, so Callie brought her father's saddle and Paul began to ride him again.

On the evenings when Anna Sheppard came up after work to help the Captain with his letters and bills, Callie came too, and sat hunched like an owl on the top rail of the fence, watching Wonderboy as he grazed, moving peacefully about the field with his head in a cloud of midges.

Everyone at the Farm was remarkable to her, because they worked there, but Paul was her hero, and her jealousy of Dora, though immature, was a more female emotion than a mere envy of her job. Paul's naturally exuberant ego enjoyed her admiration. He did not mind her dogging his heels as the schoolgirl Dora had once dogged the Captain.

Sometimes Callie's devotion was rewarded with the supreme bounty – a ride on Cobbler's Dream. In spite of her father's patient teaching, she was vague and inept on a horse, although sure of herself with them on the ground. Recognizing her uncertainty, the pony went quietly. They would amble round the meadow in the long evening sun, Callie with her eyes half closed, long back slumped under the limp brown braids, one hand trailing idly on the bright coppery coat behind the saddle flap. From time to time, Cobby would stop to turn his head and check her with his nose against her foot.

Paul watched them trot gently in one evening up the fenced

lane that led to the stable yard, Callie jogging, not bothering to rise, her mind drifted away into some far-off smiling dream. At the gateway, the pony slowed to turn into the yard, swung round too close, caught Callie's foot on the gatepost and scraped her out of her dream and on to the ground.

'See that?' Uncle shook his head admiringly. It was so long since any horse at the Farm had been ridden that he did not approve of it now. 'He done it on purpose. Baby like that shouldn't be riding him, and he knows it. Clever as a monkey. Here Cobby – coop then –' He caught the pony's bridle, but Paul, seeing that Callie was all right, took the reins away from him.

'He's not mean enough for that. He didn't see. He couldn't judge his distance.' He took the pony into his box.

'The eye? Don't scare, laddie.' Uncle hitched his Rumpel-stiltskin nose over the half door. 'Nothing wrong with him but cunning. I seen a horse once didn't like a man, and used to scrape him off on trees. He could only ride him in the open country, which made it awkward, seeing he was a gamekeeper on a big estate, all woods.'

Paul had his head under the saddle flap, taking a long time to unbuckle the girth. He did not answer. Callie came up, limping a little from fright, looked shyly at Uncle and said: 'It was my fault.'

'No ducks.'

'Yes, it *was*.' She went into the box and said: 'I'm sorry.' Paul did not say anything. He had taken off the saddle and put it over the door. He was standing with his back to her, arms round the pony's crested neck, black hair pressed against the chestnut mane, staring along the dimpled backbone at the wall behind, at nothing.

It was after this, when Cobby went into his stable in the evenings, that he began not to walk straight in with a swagger of his round quarters. He would stop on the threshold and peer into the shadows before he would step inside. Like all the horses, he always went straight to the manger, although the feeds were not brought round until they were all in from the fields. Now he did not always drop his nose right in, but would misjudge, and bump on the edge.

Paul said nothing about it, but he did not ride Cobby any more, and he told Callie to take back the saddle. When the Captain saw that he was leading the pony out to graze and in again at night, instead of letting him wander loose as before, he telephoned the vet.

'Looks as if the damage to the optic nerve has spread,' the vet said. 'The eye may stay pretty much like this, in which case he'll be able to get around, or it may go completely, in which case –'. He did not suggest: 'It might be better to have him put down,' because this was the Farm, where a horse was never robbed of life until there was no chance of its enjoying life any more.

He said: 'In which case, you'll have to look out for him. Never change his box. Put a head bumper and bandages on him for a while. Turn him out in a small field, always the same one he knows.'

The eye did not get any worse. It was still imperfect and slightly clouded, but the pony adjusted himself resourcefully to the new handicap. After a while, he did not stumble, he avoided obstacles neatly, and could go through narrow spaces as if he had grown whiskers, like a cat.

The infection in Dolly's foot had recurred twice, and it seemed that she would now be chronically lame. Another horse would have to do the small jobs which had been hers, pulling the square blue cart and the manure spreader and the machine which distributed grass seed on the overworked pasture. Dolly, when sound, was tough as old boots, and all the better for working with a light load. Among her companions, it was hard to find one who was fit to pull a doll's pram.

Old Charley the pit pony was far beyond it, and almost beyond anything else for that matter. Death or life was the Captain's decision, but he was putting this one off.

The bay Police horse, the Weaver, was also too old, and so was Trotsky, the yellow Siberian with the sawn-off head and square cow hips. Wonderboy was a steeplechaser. He would have taken off with the cart or the seeder into the next county the first time he was hitched. He was lame, in any case, and so was the brewery horse with the wet moustache, and the one-eyed gipsy mare. The donkeys, and Spot, the flat-backed circus pony were much too small, and so was the remaining Shetland, who had ceased to mourn for her over-publicised mate and taken up with the humourless mule. Willy had been a pack mule in his Army days, and was too dull-witted to be broken to harness now.

Taffy, the nurseryman's Welsh pony, was here on a month's holiday from work. Flame would have fallen down before she was ever backed between the shafts, and Pussycat had never trotted sound since the day she failed to make it to Buckingham Palace. Nero was gone in the wind, and so was Prince. Nigger, the other victim of the Night Riders, would not have even a halter on his head, let alone a bridle.

The ugly roan, Mrs Berry, was sound in wind and limb, and younger than many of the colleagues at whom he nipped, or flicked his scrubby tail and raised a sourly threatening back hoof if they came near him in the field. He was the obvious choice to wear Dolly's harness, but his doting sponsor would not hear of it. When the Captain suggested that a little work might do the old fellow some good, she flung a fringed silk stole across her face and sobbed that she had not rescued Evrémonde from the horrors of the abattoir to be a common beast of burden.

'That's probably what he was before,' the Captain said.

'Not he!' The toothsome little face, like cherry and currant ice cream, came out of the stole. 'He was a hunter. You can see it in every line. Draghounds, of course.' She drew herself up to challenge the Captain with an eye still a foot below his to suspect that in her desire for Evrémond's glory, she had forgotten the martyred fox.

Paul and Dora, who did most of the driving, did not need the surly, clumsy Mrs Berry. They had other plans. The Cobbler was beginning to get around in something like his old style. He was the youngest and fittest horse in the stable, except for his sight, and the challenge of work was the elixir of his strong spirit.

They began to break him to harness. It could hardly be called breaking. Cobby, a bold powerhouse of muscle, had never pitted his strength against a human. Even with Chrissy, he had done his willing best, although she was so rough-handed that a

84

meaner or more hysterical horse would have yanked his head down against the reins, or flung it up and reared when she jabbed him to a stop off-balance, using the bit as a weapon.

Within a week, he knew his job, backed cheerfully between the shafts, and threw his weight eagerly into the collar, leaving Dora behind if she was not quick to scramble into the cart.

Paul had taken the blinkers off Dolly's bridle, and when the pony stopped, he would turn to look for him with his clouded eye, as he used to turn and check Callie's foot in the stirrup. Paul could still make him turn round by thinking about him, and although he could not see that far, he would raise his head from the grass at the end of the field by the race-course, even before Paul whistled from the yard gate.

Ron Stryker, who liked to keep a little gentle trouble going, let it slip to Mrs Berry that Paul was neglecting the other horses for the Cobbler. He had not the nerve to say this to the Captain himself, but he knew that Mrs Berry would, since 'other horses' to her meant Evrémonde.

'If it is so,' she said, 'it's psychologically bad for him. How could he help being jealous, being in the next stable?'

'That's why he eats the door frame, I suppose,' said the Captain, who had been forced to buy copper sheathing to protect the wood from Mrs Berry's ruinous teeth.

'Of course. A deprived child will tear the wallpaper and bite his nails and chalk on the paint, won't he?' The breeze took a cherry red scarf from her throat and tried to toss it over the stable roof, but it caught on the edge of a gutter. Tiny and short-armed, she reached futilely after it. But she had dozens at home, and would make many more with each change of colour mood. 'I want you to speak to that boy about extra care. The horse should be fed first, not made to wait with all his saliva glands working. And he needs a special voice. A high French accent appeals to him, I find. *Ees beeootifool orse.* Like that.'

'I'll tell Paul,' the Captain said, and Mrs Berry went away content, leaving the cherry scarf as a bright flapping reminder on the corner of the gutter.

'Ees beeootifool orse.' The Captain tried it on the roan, and it banged up its heavy head against his nose and nearly knocked him out.

'Clumsy fool!' Paul roared at the horse, while the Captain bent over, holding his head.

Dora ran up, anxiety on her like a slap in the face. With anyone else, she might have rallied them, trying to deny the pain or injury, because she was afraid of it. With the Captain, she stood silent and put out an uncertain hand, as if she wanted to comfort him with her touch.

'Your nose is bleeding,' she whispered.

'It's not.' But it was dripping on to the cobbles, and he said: 'Oh damn,' and buried it in a handkerchief.

'You either have to lie down or sit up, I can't remember which.' Dora brought out Mrs Berry's bucket and would have flung cold water into the Captain's lowered face, but he raised his head in time, sniffed, waited, sniffed again, and the bleeding had stopped.

'Mrs Berry says you are to talk French to her horse,' he said thickly. 'You see how well it works.'

'Feel all right?' Paul stared at him blankly.

'She says you give too much attention to Cobby, and the roan is jealous.'

'Ugly clod. He don't deserve the good billet he's got.' Paul raised his arm in a mock threat to Mrs Berry, who was teetering into sleep, with his bristled eyelids half-way down like blinds.

'You're prejudiced,' Dora said. 'Cobby's Cobby. We know that. But you're supposed to love all the horses because they are horses, and need us. Not just the Cobbler because he's yours.'

'Paul thinks we're too sentimental,' the Captain said.

'I don't know. I like what you're doing, make no mistake. I wasn't brought up in this flintstone valley without learning the need for it. My grandad used to say: A horse is more use than a wife. He works harder and don't holler when you beat him. That's about the way a lot of them feel about animals – and women. But there's kids all over the world, abused and going hungry, and crazed old duffers right here in the town who get found starved to death under the arches.'

'Absolutely,' the Captain said. 'But there are thousands of people taking care of the children and the old crocks. Someone has to look out for the crocked horses.'

86

'Which comes first?' Paul frowned and kicked at the ground with his heel. 'The R S P C A man told me that his lot was started long before anyone thought of doing anything like that for children. There was this woman in New York. She wanted to report cruelty to a child in the next tenement. But it wasn't anyone's business, so she said : "All right, a child's a small animal, isn't it?" and got the R S P C A to handle it. That shamed somebody into starting a Society for the Prevention of Cruelty to Children. Seems a bit lopsided.'

'You must have Italian blood,' said the Captain. 'To an Anglo-Saxon, it would be perfectly reasonable.'

When he had gone, stuffing the bloody handkerchief into his pocket, where it might congeal for weeks before Tiny found it and dashed it into the cauldron, Dora said : 'Mrs B. is not so far out, at that. You're like people who make a big fuss of their own dog, or their own children, but kick out under the table at anyone else's. You're not really a one-track horse lover. Not like the rest of us.'

'Then what am I doing here?'

'Aren't you going to stay?'

'Do you care?' But she would show nothing in her face. 'Depends on the Cobbler. I'll stay with him. I'm God to him, you know that?'

In spite of her mother's patient, incomprehensible reasoning why there could be no one God, as such, Dora glanced round involuntarily, as if she expected to see an infuriated angel with one of those broad scimitars in the illustrations to children's Bible stories. The bolt did not strike, so she said : 'But you've got to be God to all the horses, even Mrs Berry. It's not enough if you only get worked up about cruelty when you're personally involved. The responsibility's much bigger than that.'

Ignoring the image of her Free-thinking mother, wringing her hands in the background of her mind, Dora went on : 'God is our only hope. We're the only hope of animals, once we've robbed them of wildness. Horses could kill us if they wanted to, but they make God of us, because they need us. A horse is the most dependent creature there is. We've made him so, and we have got to care, the Captain says.'

'You talk too much,' Paul said.

But soon after that, something happened which made him understand what the Captain and Dora, his echo, were trying to say. It wasn't only the Cobbler. It was all horses. All animals. Any animal who needed him.

Paul had the day off, and he decided to go and see his grandmother. He had not seen her since he ran away from his mother, more than two years ago. The shock of disappointment at finding Gran so useless when he needed her had kept him away. She might be dead by this time, or gone completely round the bend, but he was secure and content enough now to be able to face the memory of the content she had given him as a child. He would go to see her because of that.

It was a long journey. He got a ride into town in the Captain's car, and the Captain let him drive, which was a relief, for it was torture to sit in the keen little sports car with the Captain driving it as if he had a row of rich old ladies propped up in the back.

Paul had to cross town and wait an hour for the bus, and it was the same bus station where he and his mother used to wait when she was taking him back to Gran and the stables. The same grimy bus station, glass-roofed and already as dreary as a Victorian railway terminal, to which he would return dejectedly with her when she snatched him back to town. A small, hedgehog-haired boy in shrunken shorts and socks that did not match, one up to the knee, one rumpled round the ankle, dropping sullenly off the high step of the panting bus, with the face of a recaptured prisoner who has tasted freedom.

He had no idea where his mother was. Even if she had not left town, there was no reason why she should be at the bus station; but Paul sat in the farthest corner of the waiting-room with his collar turned up and a newspaper in front of his face. He did not relax until he was safely in the bus and riding through the familiar, unfamiliar streets, where so many of the shabbier landmarks were giving place to glass and concrete buildings, already starting on the inevitable process of greying towards black.

They passed through the little town where he used to change to get the bus which went past his grandfather's stables, and it was another hour before they stopped at the ugly, purposeless

village where Gran lived now with her sister-in-law. Astonishing to think that he had once walked all this way. That was
what it was to be sixteen. Couldn't do it now.

He would not be able to stay long. Even so, he would miss
the last bus from town and have to hitch a ride back to the
Farm, and Tiny would be out every half hour, flashing a
powerful torch down the road and scaring motorists that she
was the Police.

Gran was just the same, no better, no worse. Her long dark
gipsy hair was not yet grey, but streaked black and white like
the mane of a piebald horse. She knew Paul, and was glad to see
him, though not surprised. She was still quite vague about the
passing of time, and behaved as if it had been no more than a
week since his last visit.

She thought that Paul was living with his mother, so he did
not explain, for the old lady fell sad if she was corrected, and
the sweet smile which was still the garment of her face sagged
to dismay.

Her sister-in-law, who was a little slow, but a ball of fire
compared to Gran, drew Paul out to the kitchen to question
him. He told her almost nothing. She had neither seen his
mother nor heard from her, but there was always the chance
that she might, so he did not tell her where he was working, but
only that it was with old horses.

The Postman came while Paul was there, and Gran's sister-in-
law, who would have been quite social if she ever got the chance
to meet anyone, introduced them and told him what Paul was
doing. She got it slightly wrong, but near enough for the Postman to say: 'Cruelty to horses, eh? You should have been with
me at the Farm where I was today. There's a man there got an
old horse – I don't believe he's had it out of the shed for years.'
He pulled a face. 'Know what I mean? It's all you can to do go
within fifty yards of the place.'

'Why don't you tell the RSPCA inspector?'

'Not me.' The Postman shook his red head righteously. 'None
of my business. Nobody's business. It's off down a back road,
and no one goes near the place. The man comes out once and
again and gets drunk, and gets locked up for the night, and
that's about all anyone sees of him. I don't go there myself

except every six months when the rates demands are going out, and that's too often for me.'

'Did you see the horse?'

The Postman shook his righteous red head again. 'I'm not one to go prying. But I know a chap who did, must be two years ago, and he told me what he saw. Made you sick.' He pulled the face again.

'Two years ago,' Paul said. 'It must be dead.'

'It isn't then,' said the postman triumphantly, 'because I been there today, and I *know*.' He saluted the old ladies and went down the path between the straggling alyssum to his little red van.

Paul ran out after him. 'How far is it to that farm?'

The Postman grinned. Although neither he, nor anyone in the neighbourhood, wanted to get involved, it was another thing to have an outsider make their trouble for them. 'A good five miles. But hang on till I finish my round here, and I'm going back that way. I'll take you to the corner.'

Paul said good-bye to the old ladies. Gran gave him a picture of his grandfather with the big cob all rigged up for the show ring, with lamp black over the scar on its knee, and told him to be sure and come next week as usual. Her sister-in-law had forgotten about the horse, and when the red ladybird van came back, she stood on the front path with her aproned stomach propped on the low gate and waved Paul away with: 'You'll be early for the bus!'

The farm, which was only a tumbledown cottage with paper stuffed into the windows, and a collection of leering, gap-toothed sheds and pigsties, stood in a fold of the hills down a lane so badly gouged that the red mail van must have hopped from crest to crest of the deep ruts, or it would still be stuck there. Walking towards the house, Paul soon understood why the Postman had made a face. He went straight to the shed that stood in the morass of yard where a few chickens, long past laying or cooking, pecked hopelessly about in the filth.

There was no door to the narrow shed where the horse was. There had been a door, but it had broken away and was hanging round the side of the shed by one twisted hinge. The horse was not tied up, but it could not get out, even if it had been able to walk. It was standing on a platform of its own manure so high that its hind feet were almost half-way up the doorway. As the pile rose, its head had broken through the flimsy roof. It stood with the roof about its ears. It only stood because the shed was too narrow for a horse to lie down.

It was not a horse. It was a relic, a collection of bones held together with parched skin from which the hair had fallen in great patches, like a dead ponyskin coat. Only the stubborn spirit of a horse, seasoned to punishment, could have kept this creature alive for so long. The neck was a swag of bones, no more. From the barrel of the staring ribs, the taut flank was pinched up like the lean belly of a greyhound into the wasted quarters. With no muscle structure, it seemed to be all leg, but the legs no more than props, swollen with distorted joints, the hoofs twisted, pigeon-toed, from the rot within.

Paul clambered over a heap of refuse to the front of the shed where there was a small open window, through which the man apparently had put in whatever hay and water he gave the horse to keep it barely alive. Paul squeezed through the window. The filthy bed was up to the sill, and the air was thick with flies. He got up from his knees, speaking to the horse, and held out his hand.

Nostrils drawn up, lower lip trembling, eyes blank with the acceptance of nothing, the horse was barely aware of him. He put his hand under the scant mane and moved his fingers on the dry, filthy coat which would not even twitch the flies. At his touch, the horse's ears went back, as if a hand must mean a blow. Paul kept gently stroking, murmuring, and when the gaunt old head swung round at last to bump his arm, he realized that he had been crooning, like a mother with a child.

'Oh God.' His heart was flooded with a surge of rage and pity so intense that he clenched his fists and stood there for a moment trembling, his eyes closed against tears. When he opened them, the hollow, suffering eye looked into his, and he knew that the horse was his child, his treasure, his dearest care.

The rage was still there, and he scrambled back out through the window and ran to the house. The door was open and he went boldly in, ready to fight if he had to.

The cottage seemed to be just one room, and in that room all the litter of the man's living. A battered pan half full of rancid grease was in the ashes of the dead fire. Rags, yellowed newspapers, old crusts like stones, the floor a solid carpet of trodden filth, a skeleton dog no better than the horse shivering on a torn coat in the corner. In another corner, a pile of empty cans and bottles swarmed with flies.

The man lay on his back in bed, snoring. He had a stubble of beard, and it was clear from the smell – Paul made the Postman's face – that he was drunk. Paul spoke to him, and then he put his hand on the shoulder of his foul grey shirt and shook him. The man rolled over away from him with an unconscious oath, and snored again.

Paul ran. Stumbling in the twilight on the rutted lane, he ran to the road and back along it to the crossroads, where he remembered passing a small stone public house. In the tiny passage of the Dog and Fox, with the landlord and two dour beer drinkers blatantly listening through the open door of the saloon bar, Paul telephoned the Farm. He was still panting when the Captain answered, and all he could say was : 'Get the horse-box out here ! There's a horse – you've got to come out here and get him !'

'Get a grip on yourself, Paul,' the Captain said, 'and tell me the story.'

As Paul gasped out something of what he had found – he had not the words to describe the full horror of it – he could see the two dour men in the bar nodding sagely over their thick glass mugs. *They* had known about it all along. *They* could have told anyone about it, if only someone had asked them.

'But look,' the Captain said, 'even if it's as bad as you say, I can't remove the horse without authority. I'll have to call the inspector.'

'He's in London. But if he was here, you know what he'd do, and they'd use our box anyway. Please come. God knows how long that poor devil has been in there. He's half dead. He might die tonight.'

'He'll die anyway.'

'Yes, but – with us. Remember what you said about that old pony? Whatever had been done to him – and that knife-grinder had done plenty – he had that one last week of rest and food and – and love.'

'Better come home, Paul.'

'I'm not coming home without the horse.'

'All right,' the Captain said with a sigh. 'Tell me how to get there.'

They had to break down the back of the shed to get the horse out.

He was so weak that Paul and the Captain had to push his angular quarters up the ramp of the horse box, while Slugger pulled on the rope in front. It was long after midnight when they got back to the Farm. They backed right up to one of the foaling stables outside the yard, and when they got him in, his misshapen old legs folded under him, and he collapsed into the deep clean straw. When Paul brought water and a bran mash, he lifted his head to drink desperately. He slobbered the last mouthful of water over Paul's knees, and then began to eat the mash cautiously out of his hand.

Paul stayed with him all night, and Tiny came out at dawn with a raincoat over the tent of her nightdress to bring him a mug of tea. After she had seen the horse, she did not argue with him about sleeping in the stable. She gave him blankets, and her massive torch and a packet of mutton sandwiches. He stayed with the horse every night for a week, and then he sat in the straw with the tired old head in his lap while the vet centred the muzzle of the humane killer above the horse's eyes, and gave him rest for ever.

There had been no decision to make about that. It was why they had brought the half-dead horse to the Farm. Not for life, but for the gift of a humane death. But the shot in the foaling stable did not make it any easier for the Captain to decide about Charley. He hated the humane killer. He understood its mercy, but he hated it, and if he had a failing in his management of the Farm, it was, according to the more practical members of the committee, that he sometimes kept a horse alive too long.

'I'm not a sentimental man, John, as you know,' he told the vet. 'I just don't want to see Charley go yet.'

'He hasn't got much longer.' The vet was a spry, sharp-featured man like a jockey. Although his practice was mostly dogs and cats, he usually wore riding breeches and tight leggings like shiny brown drainpipes. He walked about very quickly with his hands in his pockets and his elbows working, as if he was pushing each leg forward in turn.

'What he eats isn't doing him much good,' he said, hands in breeches pockets in the pit pony's stable, keeping away from Charley's slobbery questing nose, for a hand in the pocket usually meant sugar. 'Anybody could see that. Anybody but you could see that. And that cough isn't going to get better.'

Charley coughed again convulsively, like a hypochondriacal patient trying to impress the doctor.

'Why do people cough in several syllables and animals only in one?' the Captain asked.

'Don't dodge the issue. This chap ought to go. Look at his teeth. He looks like my wife's father when his dentures are slipping. What do you say?'

The Captain looked at the rheumy old pony without answering. He knew that his time had come a few months ago, when some of the other horses began to bully him in the field, like chickens who take care of their old-age problem by pecking the senile ones to death.

The pit pony had once been black, but each time he got his winter coat, the grey hairs came in thicker, and more of them stayed behind each time he shed, so that he was now a grizzled pepper and salt, like a cheap camping blanket. He had come to the Farm from a family who had acquired him when he was already quite old, and kept him as a pet, and brought him into the house. The mother had given Uncle a photograph of Charley's shaggy head sticking out of a ground-floor window, to add to the collection of horse keepsakes in the front room of the cottage in the meadow.

He had lived peaceably among the other horses for several years. He had not tried to rule, as the Weaver did, but he had not been a whipping boy. He had always grazed alone, not pairing up for fly-swishing, head to tail, or for the pleasures of mutual neck nibbling. When the tall rangy Weaver and the small square Spot, an incongruous team, had turned against him, and began to hustle him, and nip, and back up with the threat to kick, the Captain changed his pasture. When Nero began to harry him, the Captain got a long rope and pegged Charley out on the front lawn. He could not graze, but he was content to dream in the sun, sway-backed, resting a hind foot, or to drag his rope to the shade of the tall trees that framed the garden. When the rope was wound round and round the stake, he stood with his head down, waiting patiently for someone to unwind him.

If the Captain was in the house, he made as many visits to untangle Charley as to rave at the Weaver for wind-sucking on the top rail of the fence, which he did with renewed gusto now that he had Charley on the lawn for audience. When the Captain was out, Tiny had to watch Charley's rope. 'So I am nurse-maid now to a horse, as well as to you three great helpless men.' But she would do it, grumbling at the pony, with a soft sweet biscuit for him in her apron pocket.

'He has a good life still,' the Captain said. 'I hate to take it from him.'

'My doctor,' the vet said, 'envies me because I can release my patients when they're past it and get to be a problem. It's not the patients that's the problem, I tell him. It's the owners.' He patted Charley on his thickened neck, where the coat stared dustily instead of lying sleek, and said: 'I'll stop by next week and fix up the old fellow, all right?'

He put his hand back in his pocket, and the pony arched his neck and raised a front hoof in the begging gesture somebody had taught him long ago.

'Leave it a bit,' the Captain said. 'I'll let you know.'

There had been a fresh outbreak of trouble for the horse owners in the country which lay on this side of town. The wild and wanton boys, who were known as the Night Riders – an unfortunately dramatic title which they had adopted with relish – were partly locals, but mostly from the town. They would come out on scooters and motor-bicycles, corner any horse which they found in a field or on the common land round the villages, tie anything on it for a bridle and ride it like fiends.

The horse might be found next day sweating and terrified,

exhausted, often injured. It might never be found at all. A farmer had lost a valuable brood mare one night. A woman living in the toll house had heard a clatter on the road and looked out to see a boy galloping by on a wild pale horse.

'Like Dick Turpin it was. I'd just got up to take a peep at my grandchild – she's staying with me, you see, while my daughter is confined. Her fourth, it is, and a lovely boy – when I hear this hullabaloo and there it is, like a nightmare. A big white horse with its mane and tail streaming like foam, rolling its eye, and froth flying from its mouth. When I went out next morning, there was blood on the road. Blood.'

It was a good story, and she told it many times, with embellishments. But as she described the boy differently each time, it was no more help than if she had said he was the headless horseman and let it go at that.

That was the last that was seen of the mare. She could be in the next county. She could be at the bottom of a quarry with her neck broken. A child's pony had been found wedged in a dyke with a six-inch gash inside its leg. A horse from a riding stable came back two days after it had disappeared from the yard, lame, with its wind broken.

It was after this horse was brought to the Farm in the hope that it might recover with rest that the Captain began to go out from time to time with the vigilante band of farmers and horse owners who were trying to catch the Night Riders. Often he took Paul with him, and the Captain had a shotgun, and Paul had the Captain's Army revolver, which he threw into a hedge when two policemen in a patrol car stopped to talk to them one moonlit night.

'Always seems to be worse when there's a moon, this kind of trouble,' the younger policeman said sagely.

'They're mad, that's why,' the older one said. 'Stone barmy. I talked to a boy at the station last week. Picked up trying to ride a cow. A *cow*. Poor old Jersey, full of milk. He was laughing and carrying on, and called the Sergeant sheriff. You can imagine how sweetly that went down. Said it was like the telly, and if this was the real West, no one would get steamed up about a little steer busting.' He tapped the front of his head. 'See what I mean?'

'Don't flatter them,' Paul said. 'They know what they're doing. I used to – there were boys like that where I used to live. They'd torture dogs for fun and tie cats in bags and use them as footballs. You blame it on television – crime and everything, and boys going wrong. But these mobs, when they act vicious, it's not because of the telly. It's because they like it.'

'Well, you should know,' said the policeman cheerfully, and drove off, and Paul retrieved the Army revolver from the hedge, wiped it lovingly and dropped it in his pocket. One day he would use it. From what he had heard from the vigilantes, and from something that Ron Stryker had dropped in an off moment, trying to impress, there could be boys he knew mixed up in this. It would be just the Hyena's meat. He was brutal enough for it. One day it could be the Hyena who was their quarry, and Paul would shoot him in the foot and drag him bleeding to justice. To the justice of revenge.

That night they caught two local boys of fourteen whacking a shire horse with ineffectual twigs along a back road. The Captain was elated, and whistled all the way to the police station, but when they got there, the boys protested successfully that they had found the horse wandering and were obligingly taking him back home.

Another night, when the Captain was suddenly restless and had called up the narrow stairs after Paul was in bed: 'Come on, let's go and shoot teenagers!' they had seen a boy riding along the far side of a cut and stacked cornfield. The Captain fired high to frighten the boy, and frightened the horse. It took off, leaping among the corn shocks, with the boy clinging on somehow, and disappeared into a fox covert. Paul and the Captain beat the little wood for two hours, expecting to find the boy fallen among the trees, but all they found at dawn was the hoof-marks coming out through the muddy ditch on the other side.

The boy could be anywhere by now. And the horse? The horse was found two days later ten miles down the valley, with a loop of string tied so tightly round its nose that it was embedded deeply in the flesh.

Chapter Nine

Mrs Berry was planning another trip to Ireland to buy three more doomed export horses, and she had threatened the Captain with disasters most unique if he filled up his empty loose boxes before she got back.

It would be a long trip by the time she chose the horses, got them shipped across the sea, and from Bristol to the Farm, and Mrs Berry wanted company. Her husband was not the kind of man even to consider for such an expedition, and he was in Hamburg for six weeks, which was one reason why Mrs Berry's missionary zeal was inflaming itself to a head and erupting once more across the Irish Sea. Callie Sheppard was exactly the kind of companion to take. Mrs Berry wanted Callie, and Callie was desperate to go.

They had formed a close friendship, these two, the brightly coloured little woman with the mind of a raisin and the heart of a sugar plum, and the shy pale child with the limp pigtails and searching, flecked green eyes. They lived quite near to each other, and sometimes Callie would get off the bus after school and stay for supper, and occasionally for the night, with Mrs Berry.

She was never called anything but Mrs Berry, although everyone at the Farm knew her quite well. It was as if, like her horse, she had no Christian name. Her husband must have had one for her, but no one ever saw them together. He was often abroad, arranging for the export of machinery to make machines to make machine tools, and when he was at home, all that his wife's visitors knew of him was the outside of his thick oak study door.

Mrs Berry did not mind. She led a full life of her own, spending his money on anyone and anything but herself, and whenever he was away on a long trip, like this one to Hamburg, she would launch into some special project which could be safely accomplished before he got back and found out about it.

Not that she was afraid of him. He was kind to her, as long as she kept out of his way and did not bother him; but it was his money, and although she had no qualms about spending it on grease-clogged seagulls, carted deer and worn-out horses, it made it cosier if he was not angry.

Mrs Berry did not like anyone to be angry. She was always smiling, even when she was haranguing the Captain, or poking a peacock hat out of her car window at the traffic lights to explain to a junk dealer that his pony would go better if he did not use the reins to keep his balance in the cart. Anna was not angry when she stood in the ivied porch, only determined to go through with a job she didn't like. But when Mrs Berry opened the front door – she had sent all the maids in the car to the opera, whether they wanted to go or not – she mistook the set of Anna's face for anger, and her smile collapsed so woefully that Anna had to reset her face less firmly, and knew that she had lost ground even before she stepped inside.

It was Jean who had made her come, Jean who had turned Anna's 'I don't know whether she ought to go,' into: 'Of course she can't go!'

Mrs Berry had been so good to Callie. She gave her a rare white squirrel which she had found as an abandoned baby. She bought her a blue rug for Wonderboy, with her initials in gold on both sides. She took her to the cinema, with lunch at the Royal first and tea at Bettye's afterwards, when Anna had to work in the hospital office on Saturdays.

And now the trip to Ireland. 'Oh please. Oh I beg. I'll work and work to make up when I get back. You must say yes. I've never wanted anything so much in my whole life.'

'In school time?' Jean asked, raising her black eyebrows incredulously above her swooping spectacle frames. 'You're surely not thinking of letting her go, Anna.'

'Well, I – I haven't really decided.' Anna was not concerned about the school. She believed, with Callie and Mrs Berry, that a trip like this was worth more than two or three weeks in the classroom, and if the school could not help the child to catch up afterwards, they had better go out of business. There were many things about the school which Anna did not like – the pointless rules for the sake of rules, the mediocre welfare state families who figured in the text books, the stigma if you could not climb a rope or catch a blistering cricket ball, the insistence on team spirit, when surely individualism was now the only hope for the spirit – and she often made the mistake of saying so to her daughter, which did not help Callie to like them either.

She had not immediately agreed to the Irish trip, because she thought that Mrs Berry was feckless, and capable of leaving Callie on the docks while she sailed away in triumph with her dilapidated horses. But she must not say this, must try not to seed her own opinions into Callie, to whom Mrs Berry was a faultless friend.

And so she hedged and said she had not decided, and Jean stepped in and said: 'You ought to decide right away and stick to it. It's only fair to the child.'

She was as hot on being fair as she was on being practical. It sometimes compelled her to voice truths which would be better left unsaid, pronounce drastic judgements which could have worked themselves equably out. If she ever interrupted her bureaucratic career for long enough to have children, she would probably waste hours trying to sort out who hit who first.

'What do you think, Peter?' Anna asked her son, which was rash, because before he had finished pulling his jaw sideways and down as a preliminary to speech, Jean answered for him.

'Peter thinks as I do. It would be mad to let her go.'

'Yes, but –'

'He is the head of the family, after all. Callie is his responsibility too,' Jean said crisply, and Peter nodded dependably, as if he had said it.

There was no reason why Anna should be influenced by Jean, except that she was tired and Jean never was, and she was uncertain and Jean never was, and during the four months they lived in Anna's old home together, Jean's energy and driving common sense had sapped what little resistance Anna had ever had against anybody with such an efficient grasp on life.

She went to Mrs Berry, determined to break the bad news quickly, and then lost her nerve and had to see all over the big

100

empty house and pass judgement on the new curtains in the upstairs sitting-room.

When she saw Mrs Berry in this room, My Nest, at the top of the opposite fork of the staircase from Mr Berry's study, Anna lost faith for a moment in the sight of her clear grey eyes. With the hectic curtains drawn and only one small lamp lit, the room was dim and at first there was the odd impression that Mrs Berry was camouflaged.

Then she moved to light the fire, for the autumn sun was down, and it was apparent that her blouse was made of the dizzy curtain material, and her skirt was gored with panels of chintz left over from the loose covers on the chairs and sofa.

'Do you like it?' Mrs Berry straightened up the short distance between stooping and standing and held out her skirt against the arm chair. 'I make nearly all my clothes myself. My hats too,' she added, which explained a lot. 'I hardly spend a shilling on myself. Except for shoes.' She sat down and stuck out two little feet like triangular canapés on the end of cocktail sausage legs. 'I can't make those, alas.'

Mrs Berry made tea with an electric kettle which stood in the grate, and an old toffee tin tea caddy on the mantelpiece. 'I always make it myself when I'm in my nest,' she said. 'It saves someone having to bring it up to me. My husband, you know, he asks me sometimes what do I think he pays the servants for. When I say I don't want the servants, he says I'm not fit to have all this money. But it's his fault that I have it, and since I'm not fit, I might as well give it away.'

It was not until they had had tea, with wheat germ health biscuits, that either of them said anything about the trip. Anna could not find the words to break into the chatter, and when she recognized the effort of casualness with which Mrs Berry finally referred to 'When Callie and I go to Ireland,' she knew that she was as afraid of being disappointed as Anna was to disappoint.

'Will you tell her, or shall I?' Mrs Berry asked sadly when Anna left.

'I will.' She did not trust Mrs Berry not to hypnotize herself into letting Callie think it might be all right after all.

When Anna told her, Callie was driven to cry: 'Daddy would have let me go!'

It was true. He probably would. John had been easy-going, he trusted everyone, he took chances gaily, and swept Anna along with him. It was not until she lost him that she began to be timid again, as she had been before her marriage. Callie could have said nothing that hurt more.

After Mrs Berry had left for Ireland, Jean looked up from the newspaper and said brightly: 'Terrible storms off the west coast. Aren't you glad you didn't go?'

Callie just looked at her, and chewed the end of her pigtail. Later she asked Anna: 'Was it her who said I couldn't go?'

'No darling.' Anna lied, hating to remember that she had been influenced. 'It was my decision. She doesn't tell me what to do.'

Mrs Berry kept sending postcards with pictures of bogs and power stations and breathless messages on the back. It was very exciting. She had seen two dealers and picked one mare already. White as milk. She called her Elaine. She was a lily maid. Callie should be there.

Trying to make it up to her, Anna offered Callie a treat, anything she liked.

'Why don't you take her to the circus?' Jean said. 'It starts next week at Oakshott.'

'Would you like that?'

'I wanted Mrs Berry to take me when it was at Butt's Corner, but she wouldn't. She got into trouble once for shouting out something rude to the man with sea-lions, and she daren't go again for fear her tongue will run away with her.'

'Well, you shall go.' Anna did not like circuses, but here was her chance to be one up on Mrs Berry.

'With Jean?' Callie asked doubtfully.

'No, with me. Unless Jean wants to come with us, of course.' Anna made a polite face.

Jean wrinkled her small pointed nose. 'I can't stand the smell.'

'Will you really take me?' Callie put her hands on Anna's arms and searched her eyes unblinking. 'You've always not wanted to go.'

Poor Callie. Surrounded by people with qualms and unorthodox taboos. Perhaps she should have been born into one of those smug school text-book families. *They* would go happily to the circus. *They* would never know anyone whose Mecca was the Dublin docks.

'Of course I want to go,' Anna said.

Callie had not been to a circus since she was young enough to accept it without reserve as blindingly, perfectly magical. At twelve, she could not be so easily captured by the beat and blare of the band, the jangling colour and the dramatic pillars of light, the mindless, self-hypnotizing roar of the crowd, part sadism, part laughter.

She sat quietly on a bench near the ring with her hands folded and her pigtails neatly behind her, and Anna secretly watched her face. She was not enjoying it as much as she had expected, although she turned to her mother from time to time and said: 'It's good, isn't it?' because she had wanted so much to come.

The circus was a second rate affair, with shoddy costumes and underfed animals, and most of the glamorous girls in spangles and tights were coarse and ugly and quite old when you saw them close. One dark boy with a gleaming crest of hair was fine-looking and beautiful, a swan among geese, and his stunts on the high trapeze had more brilliance and polish than anything that had gone before. But he was up in the bell of the roof too long, doing the same things to pad out the act, and Callie looked down and let her eyes wander idly over the slack-mouthed faces, craning upwards like mushrooms. She leaned forward to fiddle with her shoes. Bending down to tell her quite brusquely that since they were there, she might as well watch, Anna looked up with a lurch of fear as the whole tent rose to a gasp and the boy fell from the roof like a shot bird.

He fell into the safety net, bounced twice, and shook his beautiful black head with a grin. The fall was obviously intentional, but the crowd had had their necessary thrill of disaster, and the boy started again up the rope ladder at the corner of the net. He had a large hole under the arm of his green satin tunic. On the ground below him, just in front of Anna and Callie, a man with one eye and one shrivelled socket in the face of a punch-drunk pugilist held the rope that steadied the ladder.

Beside him, looking nowhere, and never up at the boy, stood the two men in torn and sagging sweaters who had disinterestedly tightened the turnbuckles on the guy wires when the high trapezes were swung into position before the act.

How did they get here? They looked like criminals on the run. They had the faces of brutes and the clothes of derelicts. If they tightened the wrong wire, or left a hook unclamped on the safety net, the boy would be killed. How could he trust his life to people like this?

It was one of the mysteries of the circus, as impenetrable as the mystery of why the great humble elephant should allow an elderly reconditioned blonde, with huge bruised thighs and a mouth like a sword gash, to ride into the ring on its head, poking at its face with a metal-tipped stick.

All elephants are shabby in their ill-fitting skins, but this depressed little party of four, who inexplicably obeyed the reconstituted blonde, and swung her on their trunks, and knelt for her and stood up like ponderous toys, were the destitutes of their race. As they plodded round the ring, trunk holding tail, one of them had tears falling down its sunken cheek from the small hopeless eye.

Involuntarily, Anna, who did not usually speak to strangers, turned to the woman next to her. 'I'm not surprised they've banned wild animals from the circus in Sweden,' she said. 'I wish we could do it here. Why should they hold each other's tails? It's so . . .'

The woman turned a face like a blank tombstone. 'It's quite nice for the kids, isn't it?' she said vaguely, and Anna bit her lip and looked back at the ring.

While the smallest elephant performed some humourless clowning tricks under the unceasing barrage of screams and cat-calls from the neighbourhood youth, the three larger ones wandered round the ring, their trunks roving like vacuum cleaners over the dirty trodden sand, picking up toffee papers and lolli-pop sticks and putting them thoughtfully into their mouths. When they finally shambled out, their back views stooped like the shoulders of defeat, one of them, the one who was crying, had a crumpled paper cone that had held candy floss sticking out of the side of his mouth like a wayward tooth.

Callie had not spoken while the elephants were on. As they shambled out, she said, without looking at Anna: 'An elephant's brain is four times as big as a person's. They don't have to let her do that to them.'

Anna did not say anything. Everyone else seemed to be having a good time. If you did not like circuses, you were a crank. Callie must decide for herself.

However, when the barred cage was locked into place by the same unprepossessing men who had fixed the trapeze, Anna found that she could not keep quiet about the lions.

They slunk into the cage, half doped and mangy. There were bald patches of scrofulous skin on the bodies that swung listlessly on to the high, undignified stools. On some of them, the moulting hair hung in dirty matted ropes from their shoulders and breasts, tangling with their abject stride.

The lion-tamer, unaccountably wearing the uniform of a Canadian Mountie, was inside the bars, wielding a kitchen chair and firing blanks from a small pistol to stimulate the excitement which was lacking in such a dejected gathering of cats with drawn teeth. One of them was trained to lunge at him, and the trainer would throw the chair at the lion and run through a sliding door which was pulled open for him by one of the ruffianly men outside, and shut in the nick of time as the lion hurled itself against the bars with a roar that was echoed two octaves higher by the audience. This was repeated two or three times to impress the danger of it. The Mountie goaded the lion. The lion leaped with a roar and a slash of claws, and the one-eyed man slid open the escape door just in time to let the fearless trainer out.

When it had been established that only this swift work with the emergency door preserved the Mountie for the next performance, One-eye casually left his vital post to push a hurdle through the bars, and to the accompaniment of a staccato of pistol shots, the same man-eating lion was called from his stool to roll over like a dog and jump back and forth across the hurdle with a lithe grace which no amount of dope or misery could conceal.

'I wish it would kill him,' Anna said quite loudly. Several people turned to stare at her, and a man in the front row swung

105

sharply round with the same kind of face he would have shown to anyone who vilified the Queen.

'You hate it, don't you.' Callie whispered. 'Why did you come?'

'I came to please you.' Wretched and guilty, because she had sat and watched the humiliation of the elephants and the lions, and paid money which would enable the acts to continue, Anna hoped that Callie would say: 'I hate it too,' but she was silent. One of her pigtails was forward over her shoulder and the end was in her mouth.

But when the horse came on, the terrible thin brown horse with the white face, while people were still chuckling over the clowns with the flour and the buckets of water, Anna no longer cared whether she made a crank out of her child. She had to make her hate it.

The horse was old and lack-lustre, with angular hips and a bridle too big for him, so that the spangled browband came down too far over his eyes, like an oversize hat.

As he performed his few jerky dancing steps, and turned, and stepped high to the music, he looked as if he had once been well trained, and could not forget. But he was afraid. Not of the crowd or the raggedly blaring band, but of the girl who rode him.

She sat stiffly, in blue satin trousers and top hat, with a steely smile and eyebrows drawn like crowbars. The horse wanted to please, but his eye was rolling back to the girl and his ears twitched back in distrust, and when he made a mistake because she gave him the wrong signal, she yanked at the rein to turn him, and he threw up his bony old head to escape the pain of the long vicious curb.

'He hates her,' Anna said tensely. She found that she was sitting forward, gripping the wooden bench.

Callie said with a sigh: 'I hate her too.'

Now they were in committed union, the two of them. Now they were as one against the indifferent crowd, who were bored with the equestrian act. At the end, after the horse had counted with his front hoof, to the unconcealed snap of the girl's switch against his leg, and then sat like an ungainly mongrel with his tail spread out in the dirty sand, the girl remounted and tried

106

to make him lie down with her on top. You could see the old bones gathering themselves to respond in the remembered way. He sagged at the knees, his legs quivering, his shoulder too stiff, trying to obey; but she had his head pulled so far round, with his white nose touching her boot, that it was impossible for him to get right down.

The drums kept rolling. The horse kept trying, awkward and afraid, the girl's hard face grew harder. At last she jerked him up and rode out of the ring to thin applause, and Anna and Callie knew by her face that she was going to beat the horse.

They were both too upset to stay. On the way out, they passed the canvas tunnel where the stalls for the horses and elephants were. The brown horse was tied to a pole with his saddle and bridle still on, and his head down as if he had been ridden all day.

'Let's go and talk to him,' Callie said, but a gross man squatting on an upturned bucket gave Anna a sour, intimidating glance and she pulled the child away.

They went to the car and Anna drove in silence, pushing back tears. Callie sat with her head down and her hands hanging between her knees. She did not speak until they were nearly home. 'He looked at me,' she said, and the eyes she raised to her mother were wide and shocked. 'He looked at me.'

If only Mrs Berry were here. She would have helped. She would have risen to the challenge like boiling caramel and done something about it, like the time she had stormed into the pet shop and bought the blindly shivering monkey in the window.

The monkey had died three days later, rolled in an eiderdown in the armchair by Mrs Berry's bed, but it would have died anyway in the shop, and the brown horse would die if it had to stay in the circus.

It would die of a broken heart, and there was no one but Callie to save it. He looked at me. With that sad, gaudy bridle sagging on his brow he looked at me. Come back, Mrs Berry, oh please come back. I need you. It was you who taught me to feel like this, as if it were my fault, mine to put right.

'Do you suppose,' she asked her mother, tossing it off as if she did not care one way or another, 'that the girl would sell us that horse from the circus?'

'Oh dear.'

Anna thought that she had influenced her daughter to mind about the animals in the circus, but Callie had started to mind first. Right at the beginning, when the bear was waiting to come on in the parade, she saw him flop back on all fours when the man was not looking, and saw the craven defeat with which he heaved upright again when the man turned round. She had kept silent, since it was she who had wanted to come to the circus, to recapture remembered delight. But where was that clapping baby of five years ago, who had sat entranced and seen nothing wrong?'

'I was just talking,' she said. 'It doesn't matter.'

'It does.' Anna frowned. 'But you know we haven't got the money.'

Callie knew. It was what she had known she would hear. When you were poor, it was about all you did hear.

She went boldly to the Captain, to tell him about the horse and its humiliation. But her boldness evaporated before she reached him, and she told it badly, she knew she did. A sucker for a sad story, Paul had said, but she could not make her stammered story sad enough. Clasping her hands tight to her and bending over them as if she had stomach pains, she tied her words in shy knots, not knowing how to make him see.

'I don't like circuses either,' he said, 'but thousands of people do.'

'I know. That's why it was so terrible. My mother and I – we got up and left, and people stared. And then I saw the horse again afterwards, and he – oh please – you've got to take him away!'

'Got to? Got to? My dear girl, I can't.' The Captain looked down at her with one side of his face screwed up as if he had been kissed by the Bearded Lady.

'You took that horse Paul found with its head through the roof.'

'That was different. I knew the man was bound to be prosecuted. As it was, I got into trouble for taking it without authority, when the man was too drunk to know. I'm not going

108

to be talked into anything like that again. Don't get fussed Callie,' he said with a gentle drop to his voice. 'It's probably not as bad as you think.'

'It is.' She blinked and bit her lip. 'I've seen it. I can't report it. People don't take any notice of a child. But you could. We could go and rescue it. It isn't very far. I'd come with you – if you'd take me.'

'Of course I would.' But his smile was for a child, not a partner in a crusade. 'But you know, if I went round removing horses from everyone who can't ride, I'd have half the horses in the country at the Farm.'

'She's cruel,' Callie said. 'He hates her.' She looked down at her blunt worn sandals and the Captain's weatherbeaten brogues, toe to toe on the cinder path. 'You could buy the horse.'

'It's not my money, you know. I could make an investigation, but the committee would have to decide.'

The committee! She knew about committees. Jean talked about them all the time. 'It's got to be now. The circus is moving on the day after tomorrow. They're going to Scotland.'

'We'll see,' the Captain said kindly. 'We'll see.'

We'll see. Who but a grown-up ever said that? Who but a child ever understood the urgency of Now? 'Oh, I wish Mrs Berry was here!' she cried.

'Perhaps,' said the Captain, 'it's just as well that she's not.'

He smiled, and Callie turned and ran, although she heard him calling her back. If he was going to be funny about it, then that was the end. He was out of it. Now there was only Callie.

The night before the circus left, the rain came down straight and steady, soaking earth and air.

Raining! Callie pulled her head in from the window and slumped on the wide sill. Every time she had ever wanted anything more than life, it was raining. Last year at school when she had a chance for the hundred yards. The camping trip with Dad. The day he was going to let her lead Wonderboy in the paddock at Plumpton and she had a cough. Well, all right, it would be better with no moon, and the rain would keep people indoors. Dogs indoors. The bad fairy in blue satin would be holed up somewhere in a moulting marabou négligé. The fat surly man on the bucket would be in a caravan, snoring on his back. Callie would get soaked through and catch pneumonia and then everyone would be sorry.

Mrs Berry would be sorry she had gone to Ireland without her. The Captain would be sorry that he had treated her like a child. Her mother would be sorry ... sorry for what? Callie paused on the stairs and then shrugged and stepped on down in her socks. She would be sorry for not being the kind of daring mother who could share the secret.

And for having a child who was not daring either. In trousers and a dark sweater to blend with the black night, Callie crept through the kitchen where the neurotic cat which Jean despised was lying on the ironing board like a patient on an operating table.

'This isn't me,' Callie whispered, touching for good luck its narrow head which it immediately shook with a sound like flapping leather, nervous of its ears. 'It's someone terribly brave and cocky.'

It's Paul. He would not do a thing like this unless he knew it could be done, and if he knew it could be done, it could.

I'm Paul. Scared half-witless by the creaking door of the shed, Callie got out her bicycle and rode through the rain with her head down, as if that would keep her dry.

Paul woke up when the Cobbler neighed, dropped back into sleep for a moment, then woke as he neighed again, and sat up. Another horse called, Dolly's unmusical baritone. Paul knew the sound of all the horses. The mares were deeper, and Mrs Berry had that hoarse strangled bellow, like a bronchial ass.

The Cobbler again. When he first came, he used to call sometimes at night, challenging his surroundings, flinging a sudden cry to a lost stablemate. Now he never called until the cockerels set him off, or he saw Paul in the dormer window waving the curtain at him.

Paul got up and looked out, but the rain was bringing the clouds down with it in a dripping mist, and he could not see as far as the stables. He put on some clothes and went out barefoot. The top doors of the loose boxes were shut, for the autumn

110

nights were uncertain and the old horses had little resistance to a sudden drop in temperature. Paul spoke softly, opened the corner door and found the pony's nose where it always was when he opened up in the morning: right against the crack of the door, ready to nudge him with a rough caress on the side of his neck.

He seemed all right. Paul shut the door again and stood for a moment listening to the sounds of him moving round the stable, rustling, nosing the manger reminiscently as he passed, gleaning a last wisp of hay, crunching it, stopping to listen, crunching again. Every line of him, every movement, every look in his eye and ear were as clear to Paul as if he were inside the stable, as if he himself were the pony.

The noisy teeth stopped again to listen. A horse blew down its nose in the foaling stable behind the barn outside the yard. Paul's feet were cold on the puddled cobbles, and his wet hair was streaked into his eyes. He was turning to go when he realized that there had been no horse in the foaling stable since he had kept his bony old friend company in there before he was put to sleep.

Of all nights for the Captain to prowl, he would have to choose this one. He might have been woken by Cobby. He might have been normally restless. He might have got up to look at the premature puppies.

The Cobbler called again while Paul was talking desperately to the Captain in the blanketing rain, steering him away from the lane. If Hero answered, all was lost. Soaked, shivering, mud to the knees, her feet like clogs, Callie pinched the bone of his nose until he snored like a dragon and threw up his head. Cold on the back of her neck, she imagined the impact of the Captain's voice. If it went wrong now, after what she had done, it would feel like being shot. Callie stumbled on through the mud, tugging the slow brown horse, her cold face dripping with rain and tears.

She walked into the yard arrogantly, in a pair of cracked red Russian boots and a flared belted coat with the collar turned up. She could have been quite good-looking, but her face was as hard and sour as early cherries, and when she smiled, which she did hastily when she saw Paul, she showed two gold teeth and a lot of dubious ones.

Paul and Slugger Jones and Dora were cleaning stables. Paul was the farthest from the archway, but the blonde went straight to him. 'Oh, hullo there,' she said, trying hard.

'Hullo.' Paul went on shaking out straw, tossing the wet part into a wheelbarrow and the clean in a pile against the wall of Mrs Berry's loose box.

'I've lost one of my horses.' The girl stood on the other side of the barrow, boots apart, hands in pockets. 'I thought someone here might have seen him.'

Paul shook his head and went on working in silence, and she said: 'They do sometimes run to where there's other horses, so I'm trying all the places round about where we are. With the circus, you know.' Her accent was cautious, single sounds delicately tortured into two genteel vowels.

'That so, Miss?' Paul straightened up, leaned on his fork and gave her one of his charmers, and she flashed the gold teeth. 'Liberty horse, is it?'

'It's a high school act. Dressage.' She rhymed it with message. 'I studied under the late Colonel Rubinsky.'

'Lucky you,' Paul said, although the Colonel sounded as if she had made him up.

'I have two very highly trained horses. At least I had, until this morning. When the boy went out to feed them, Moonstone was gone from the tent. Just disappeared.'

'You sure you tied him properly?'

'I don't take care of my horses myself,' she said distantly, drawing her silver blonde head back into the high collar. 'But the boy swore he'd tied him as usual. The rope was still across the poles behind him, so he must have got under it somehow and gone off in the rain. I can't understand it. He's got loose before, but never gone far from the others. He may have been stolen.'

'Have you told the Police?'

'For what it's worth. You know what country coppers are.' Her lofty urban smile was a glittering sneer. 'It takes a bomb to shift them, and we're moving on tonight, to Aberdeen of all

God-forsaken places, and I must find Moonstone. They told me about this place, so I came here first.'

'He's not here, if that's what you mean.' Paul challenged her hint belligerently and a mottle of blue and red crept up her neck – she wasn't the type to blush – and she said with a grim mouth: 'I didn't say so. I thought you might have seen a loose horse.'

Paul shook his head, moved the barrow and came out of the stable. 'Dora!' he called. 'You seen a loose horse anywhere? Lady here's lost a horse.'

'Oh,' said Dora, coming up, 'how exciting. You're that blue woman from the circus. I went the first night with some girls from the village. I saw you.'

The blonde waited for her to say something good about the act, but Dora only asked: 'Is it the black horse or that thin brown one that wasn't very good?'

Paul laughed and bit it off, and the blonde jerked the in-artistically drawn eyebrows together across the top of her high-bridged nose. 'It's Moonstone,' she said coldly, 'and he's dark bay, for your information. He's a very valuable horse, and he's got loose.'

'I don't blame him,' said Dora cheerfully. 'It's a dreadful life for an animal, being in the circus. Doing tricks for all those gaping apes, and here today and gone tomorrow. Does she think we've got him?' she asked Paul.

'Maybe we have. There's so many here, I lose count. You want to look round, Miss, and see for yourself?'

The blonde hesitated, looking from Paul to Dora suspiciously. Then she said: 'I'll let the Police do that.'

A horn sounded imperatively from the road, and she said: 'I mustn't keep my friend waiting out there. Home of Rest for Horses. He'll think they've taken me in.'

Liking her for the joke, Paul was sorry that he had teased her and let Dora blunder into rudeness. He gave her a nice sincere look from his blue eyes and said: 'I wish we could have helped. It's tough luck on you,' but she rejected the look and the sympathy by flipping Mrs Berry on his strawberry nose and saying: 'That's the ugliest horse I've ever seen. Why on earth do you keep all these old wrecks alive?'

When she had gone, with the inferior roar of a small cheap engine with the silencer taken off to make it sound like a sports car, Dora said to Paul: 'You've got the horse here.'

'How do you know?'

'I can tell when you're lying. If you didn't know anything about it, you'd at least have told her you'd seen it running loose. You always lie.'

'Only to people like her.'

'Where's the horse?' Dora gripped his arm. 'Oh, I am glad. He was tragic at the circus and she was vile. I've been worried about him ever since.'

Paul jerked his head. 'He's in the old shed at the bottom of that little boggy field the other side of the wood.' He drew a finger across his throat. 'My knife if you tell.'

'Someone will find him.'

'Not yet. And the circus will be gone. It'll work out. Moonstone,' he chuckled. 'She calls him Hero. That's almost worse.'

'Who does?'

'Callie. She brought him here.'

'Callie? She couldn't have.'

'She did then. And it's the knife again if you tell her I told you. She wants it to be just me and her.'

The circus packed up its tents and moved out of Oakshott that night, leaving only a morass of trampled wet earth and paper at the end of the common. The blonde had apparently gone with them, and when Anna came up to the Farm to do the letters, Callie came with her, visited Wonderboy only briefly with carrots, and disappeared for an hour.

'Where have you been?' Dora asked, to see what the child would say.

'Collecting plants,' said Callie, and walked on towards the house. She could not lie like Paul and look you full and smiling in the face.

'New hobby?'

'It's for school.'

Dora was aching to tell that she had gone down through the muddy fields to see Hero before dawn, and to share the adventure with her. She had not promised . . . 'Callie!' She stepped

114

after her, but Callie called out: 'I have to go!' and ran on into the house.

Dora went out to the top meadow and talked to Flame, who was dreaming near the fence, uninterested in the waning, wintery grass. She could always think better with her hand on a horse. After a while, she decided that she was glad that Callie had not stopped. Suppose it was not so much that she wanted to share the adventure as that she was jealous because Callie shared it with Paul? If her mother knew that she was capable of being jealous of a twelve-year-old child, she would have her psycho-analysed.

The Police did not come for a few days, and when they did, one of them was a friend of the Captain's and had been in court with him on some cruelty cases, and had once pulled him out of a fight with three men in the market who were sitting on the head of a frantic unbroken three-year-old.

The boggy field below the wood was not being used, and the Captain said quite truthfully that he knew nothing about the missing circus horse. He would keep his eyes open for it if he went out again with the vigilantes, but the Night Riders had been quiescent since the weather got bad, and he had not been out after them for weeks.

It was Ron Stryker, of course, who told the Captain. It had not taken him long to find out about Hero. His long experience of spying for all sides and trusting none had developed his instinct for funny business, however well concealed. He missed nothing. A cryptic word, a look between Paul and Dora. The way Callie walked when she came back from the wood with her half-hearted bundle of meaningless weeds. A little guesswork, a little investigation, a little deduction, and he had it pat.

The Captain sent for Paul. 'Bring in,' he said, 'that thin brown horse with the white blaze.'

'What thin brown horse?' Paul's eyes were very wide, very blue between the curling black lashes. 'Old Puss? I wouldn't call her thin. Her belly –'

'All right. I'll get him myself.'

Paul looked at the Captain and then he looked away. 'Too sticky down there,' he mumbled. 'I'll get him.'

*

The Captain was angry when he came to Anna's house. Tiny had told him to wait until he cooled down, but he had brushed her off, climbed into his sporty little car, fought with the starter and gears, and jerked off down the hill with his blood still up.

He found Anna and Jean together in the big shabby central room where everything happened except sleeping and bathing and cooking. If he had been calmer, he might have waited until he got Anna alone, for girls like Jean unnerved him. As it was, he burst out as soon as Callie had let him into the house: 'Do you know what your daughter has done!'

Callie had escaped upstairs. 'What?' asked Anna faintly, putting a hand behind her to feel for a chair in case her legs let her down.

The Captain told her. He made it sound like nothing more than stealing, which technically it was, and Anna cried out: 'Oh, poor Callie! It's all my fault.'

'She's twelve,' the Captain said. 'She ought to have her own ideas of right and wrong by now.'

'She has.' Anna did not sit down. She stood with her hands pressed flat against her skirt and her small fair head poked forward, shooting words at him. 'But she's got ideas of courage too, which is tremendous, when you're not born brave to start with. If she really did what you say she did, I think it's magnificent.'

'Magnificent,' said the Captain disgustedly. 'What a way to bring up a child. You can take anything you want, if you've got nerve enough. Why doesn't she rob a bank? That boy would help her, I've no doubt.'

Jean was silent, watching intently from the background the fascinating spectacle of these two quiet, friendly people suddenly at war.

'You can leave Callie out of it,' Anna said, her pale face reddening. 'And Paul too. I told you, it was my fault. It was I who encouraged her to be sorry for the horse. She's soft-hearted anyway, and I played on that, instead of trying to make her enjoy the circus, like everyone else did.'

'She came to me, you know, and tried to rope me in. But I

116

could see she was exaggerating wildly, like all crusading women.'

'Perhaps not. You didn't see the horse. It was having a bad time.'

'I've seen it now. It's a perfectly healthy animal. A little poor, but nothing on it to indicate abuse. Too old for the job, perhaps, but aren't we all?'

'You didn't see him with the girl. He hated her.'

'Oh!' The Captain ran his hand through what there was of his hair. 'You women are all the same. This job's taught me that, if nothing else. You flatter yourselves you're so compassionate, but half the time it's no more than thoughtless sentiment. And so you teach your children to be sentimental. Without reasoning, without logic. Just sentimental.'

'You're just as bad!' Anna found herself saying, as if mercy and kindness were insults.

'Look here,' said the Captain, 'if I thought I was as sentimental as a woman, I'd shoot myself and all the horses at the Farm.'

'What do you know about women?'

'Enough.'

Their voices had risen together to a peak of noise and they suddenly realized that they were shouting, and fell silent all at once, staring at each other with closed, intractable faces. Callie, who had been listening outside the door, peered round it at the silence, and then crept in and stood uncertainly, looking from one to the other.

'Oh please don't fight about me,' she whispered at last. 'It was all my fault.'

'You mustn't take all the blame.' Jean came in crisply, sensing her opportunity. 'Something like this was bound to happen, Anna,' she said, and Anna turned in surprise at the hostility in her voice, for she thought that even incompatible families would always stick together under outside attack.

'I've always said you try to influence her too much.' Jean stood with her hands behind her and her chin up, as if she were testifying faith and not disloyalty. 'A child has to develop its own ideas about life. You've got so many quirks and aversions, and you're always trying to impose them on her.'

'I – I don't think I do.' Anna fumbled for words, looking

down and stammering, not because she was nonplussed by Jean, but because she was ashamed for the Captain to see her being bullied by her daughter-in-law. A feeble character he would think her; less fit than ever to bring up a child.

'You lost her a friend at school because Callie told the girl you said her father was a murderer if he shot pheasants.'

'I said it was murder in general. I didn't say anything about her father.'

But Jean went on without listening: 'You put all these ideas in her head, and now look what you've made of her. A thief.'

Anna stared and could not answer. Callie began to cry. The Captain, who had turned from Anna to Jean and had been coming slowly up to the boil while she spoke her mind, cleared his throat of the accumulated choler and told her jerkily: 'Look here, the child is your sister-in-law. That's a terrible thing to say.'

'It's the truth,' Jean said flatly. 'No one in this house ever faces the truth.'

'I do,' the Captain said more boldly. 'I think I'm beginning to see the truth.' He seemed to have transferred his anger from Anna and Callie to Jean. When she put her oar in, he had to scull on the other side. 'The child thought she was doing the right thing. That's why she did it. Now I'm wondering how she did it. It was quite a feat.'

'A feat!' Jean's laugh was scornful, her spectacles like the make-up of the wicked Queen in Snow White. 'All right,' she said, 'tell us. How did you do it, Callie?'

'How? I – oh, I –' Callie had stopped crying when she saw that the Captain was suddenly on their side. She answered Jean's question to him. 'It was easy. I just imagined I was someone else.'

'Who?'

Callie hesitated. 'Someone brave. Then I wasn't even scared. Yes, I was. The rain was in my eyes and it was dark and I fell over a tent rope and thought I'd broken my ankle. In films someone always breaks their ankle at the critical moment and the others have to decide whether to leave them to die or risk their own lives to go back and carry them. They always go back, at

118

least the good side do. That's one way you can tell which side is which. But I didn't have any others, and I thought I would lie there in the rain with my face in the mud and they would get a gun out of one of those booths where it's a shilling for six tries at clay ducks that won't fall over, and shoot me.'

'She's making it up.' Jean lit a cigarette and perched on the arm of a chair, amused.

'I'm not. How could I imagine myself doing any of this if I hadn't actually done it? No one came, so after a bit I got up and found I'd only banged my ankle on the iron tent peg. I went to where the horses were. It was only two sides and a roof, no ends to it, and they were cold and shivery, tails tucked in, heads down and miserable, as if they'd eaten the last wisp of their hay hours ago. I wanted to take them all. I took Hero – that's his name now, whatever she called him – and I hooked the rope back across where he'd been, so they'd think he got untied and sneaked under it. Getting out of that tent, and thinking all the time someone would hear us, I'd have died if it hadn't been for him. I was afraid before, alone, but with him, it was as if he was leading me, instead of me him. He was so gentle. He is the most gentle horse I ever knew. I thought a dog would bark and hundreds of people would come spilling out of all the caravans. I thought floodlights would suddenly go on and sirens wail like when someone escapes from prison.'

'Those Saturday afternoons with Mrs Berry at the cinema have not been wasted, I see,' Jean said in what her youth and conceit mistook for a sophisticated voice.

Callie glanced at her pityingly and went on: 'If Hero and I were caught, I was going to say I'd found him loose and was bringing him back. Like you told me the Night Riders said when you caught them with that plough horse,' she reminded the Captain, and Anna could not help saying: 'It seems I'm not the only one who gives children ideas.'

She looked sideways at the Captain, to see if he would be angry again; but he laughed, so she laughed too, and Callie let out a great sighing gust of breath, because it was done now, told. She had unloaded the dangerous weight of her secret adventure, and no one had done anything but laugh.

Except Jean. She heard Peter's car, and went out to give him

her version of the story before anyone else could get at him
with theirs.

The Captain watched her out of the door, callously, like a
cat, then shifted his gaze back to Callie. 'You were very brave.'

'Then will you keep Hero?' She pounced.

'I'm sorry. He'll have to go back.'

'He can't!' Callie raised clenched hands, and if she had been
a different kind of child, she would have beat on him like a
door that will not yield. Shaking the tense fists that were afraid
to touch him because she had been too long without the physical
contact of a father, she cried: 'If you could see that terrible
girl – if you only could have seen her! Now it's too late.'

The Captain thought for a moment, considering her passion,
and then he rotated his shoulders inside the tweed jacket and
said: 'Is it? Perhaps I will.'

'But she's in Aberdeen.'

'If she can get there, so can I,' the Captain said with the
courage of one who never went farther than London, and then
only if the Committee refused to come to him.

'You don't mean –' Callie was afraid to hear the answer – 'in
the horse-box with Hero?'

'Not yet. First I'll see his owner. I must at least reassure her
that the horse is safe.'

'You could write that,' Anna said. 'What are you planning?'

'I'll see when I get there,' the Captain said.

Chapter Ten

The Captain was in Scotland when Mrs Berry arrived from Ireland with her horses, which was just as well, since Hero was in one of the empty boxes and Mrs Berry's bent-kneed skewbald had to go in the foaling stable.

She fussed so much about him being lonely, and disappointed with his accommodation after what she had promised him, that Uncle changed him with old Charley, who was just as happy to dream and dribble alone.

While her three new horses settled in at the Farm, Mrs Berry was constantly there to check on their condition, reassure them, and cultivate their comradeship. She hung on their doors, worshipping, clucking, feasting her eyes on the stolid black, the nervous grey with the scarred face, the rickety skewbald who looked like an old iron bed without the mattress. Sometimes she would go in and sit on the edge of the manger – her legs were so short that she had to climb on an upturned bucket to get there – and croon and caress the ancient heads.

Going in one evening with the skewbald's feed, Paul found Mrs Berry perched in the corner shadows like a plump macaw. He had to lift her down from the manger, and she wriggled and squeaked as she landed in the straw, and rolled her eyes up at him and cried: 'Oh my, you are strong!' Normally she was not a bit like that, 'but she's in love with the horse,' said Dora, 'and some of it rubbed off on you.'

Mrs Berry had looked forward eagerly to showing Callie her new horses, and retailing in all colourful detail what she had been through to get them here. For Callie it would be second best to going on the trip. It would give her some part in it, and Mrs Berry was planning to offer her half shares in whichever of the horses she liked best.

It was very disappointing to find Callie so wrapped up in the circus horse that she would scarcely do more than glance over the doors of the newcomers and remark about the broad black cob: 'He doesn't look like a refugee,' before she dragged Mrs Berry across the yard to see Hero.

'If you had been there,' she said with shining generosity, 'you could have rescued him.'

'But then I would not have rescued Lancelot, Guinevere and Elaine.'

'Oh them,' said Callie and went into Hero's stable and laid her face against his meagre ewe neck, drank in the heady smell of him and promised him he should not go to Aberdeen.

When the Captain came back, he did not say anything at first to Anna and Callie, and they did not like to ask. When it was Anna's evening to go up to the Farm, she did not take Callie, in case it was bad news.

The Captain came in to the office and dictated letters in his usual manner, which was to say vaguely: 'Tell her she's all wet – you know the tactful way to do it,' or: 'Tell him No – but kindly,' or: 'Thank them. Second grade thanks. It was only half a sack of carrots after all, and they send a truckload to market every day.'

He was rather brisk and businesslike today, a little jaunty, and he soon went out and left her. It was not until Anna had had her coffee and cake and a long chat with Tiny about Paul's manners and Slugger's chest, that the Captain came back, when she was almost ready to go.

'I forgot to tell you,' he said abruptly. 'Callie's horse can stay.'

'Oh, thank you! Oh, I don't know how to –'

'Nothing to it.' He screwed up the side of his face as he did when he was not sure how to react to emotion. 'He shouldn't be here, of course. He's not that much of a crock, and if you ever get a stable again, Callie can take him away and ride him, but he can stay meanwhile. I'll try to square it with the Committee.'

'I can never thank you enough.'

'Not me. It was that girl. She was very nice.' He raised the eyebrow that worked, and grinned.

'She can't have been.'

Anna was sitting in his chair behind the desk, and he stood opposite, leaning forward across the typewriter. 'When we were having that fight at your house,' he said, 'one of the quite nasty things you said to me was: "What do you know about women?" All right. What do *you* know? She was very nice. I had a good time. I took her out to supper. Don't drop your jaw at me. You think I'm not the kind of man who takes circus ladies to supper?' He took his hands off the desk and stood up. 'Well, you're right. But she took me, really. I mean, I paid, of course, but it was her –' He was suddenly quite embarrassed, and went to stand by the window, as if he had the excuse of looking out for the Weaver cribbing on the fence; but the Weaver was in his stable long ago, cribbing on the manger.

'I know what you mean,' he said, looking out across the darkling lawn, where a straggled line of dead uncut chrysanthemums rattled in the wind. 'She is a sort of daunting person when you first see her. I had written and asked her to meet me in a hotel – I didn't want to get mixed up with the circus – and when she walked into the lounge, all bust and boots, I thought Good God, I'm for it, and I almost turned and ran. Officer and gentleman, I told myself. Stand firm. She didn't want tea, so we had a drink, which was what she'd already had, and when I caught the whiff of that, I thought that she might have been as scared of me as I was of her, and needing courage.'

'I don't see why she should be scared,' Anna said. 'Oh – not that you aren't impressive, but she was on the right side of the Law.'

'She didn't know that. We had a couple of drinks and both talked round the subject, and then she had another one and started to relax, and she let it out that she thought I'd come to investigate her treatment of the horses. There had been some complaints before, apparently – you and Callie weren't the only ones – and all of a sudden, she began to cry. It must have been the gin, because she's not the type to cry when strictly sober, but it touched my heart, the mascara running and so on, and so I told her the truth.'

'You promised you wouldn't tell her what Callie did.'

'I mean just half the truth. I told her that I had the horse, but I said that I'd found it wandering and that it had cut its leg

123

badly, and in any case I thought it was in very poor condition and shouldn't be worked.'

' "My livelihood!" I was afraid she was going to cry again, although she had stopped to listen to me. I said I would be glad to buy the horse. "But Moonstone was trained!" She set up a wail, and so I offered her a hundred and fifty pounds for him, which shut her up cold like a slap across the mouth.'

'It was after that we went out to supper. She pretended to be very sentimental about the horse – trying to push me up on the price, I thought. So when she'd finished drooling into the fish about the horse being man's best friend, I asked her if she was quite satisfied, and she said – you know what she said?'

'She wanted more, I suppose.'

The Captain shook his head and giggled. 'She leaned all over me and the fried plaice – we were on to the wine by then – turned up her globular eyes and said: "To tell you the truth, Captain dear, I only gave forty pounds for him".'

'Callie and I will never be able to thank you,' Anna said. 'One day we'll pay you back for Hero, but we'll never be able to thank you.'

'Oh hush.' The Captain had been standing with his back to the window, leaning on the sill while he talked to Anna. He turned away now to look out again at the garden. 'If I'd paid more attention to Callie in the first place, she wouldn't have got mixed up in this. It proved what she could do though.'

'But she left you with the mess.'

'I enjoyed it. Noreen and I – that's her name, Noreen – we had a good time. She – she took a liking to me.'

He sounded surprised, so Anna said to his back: 'Why not? You're very likeable.'

'Oh hush,' he said again, and gave the impression of turning up his coat collar, although his hands stayed on the sill. 'I'm just a cranky old bachelor. People round here call me That crank with the horses. Apart from keeping animals alive who can't work, I'm odd man out because I haven't a wife.'

Anna clasped her hands on the desk and looked down at them because she did not want to look at the Captain, in case he turned round and saw her face. She knew too well what he meant. Less than a year since John died and already she knew, in the homes of certain unimaginative friends, the feeling of being an outcast among couples.

'They produce unmarried sisters and cousins, worthy old girl friends who've never had a man. It's pathetic, some of the women they've tried to marry me to. Tiny says I'm married to the horses. I suppose she's right. I was almost married once though, six years ago before I left the Army.'

Anna kept quiet. She had learned long ago that silence, not questions, was the only way to learn anything. Outside the cone of light from the desk lamp, the room was in shadow, the Captain vague by the window. A mountainous ghost came out of the side door and floundered about on the wintry lawn. Tiny in her white baking apron, calling to one of her cats. It came to her from the hedge, galloping with its tail straight up, and she swooped and turned back, and the rectangle of light from the door narrowed to a pencil shaft and went out.

As if he could not talk even within sight of the possessive woman, the Captain waited until the door banged – Tiny never shut a door.

'She was much younger than me. Roxanne. Younger and cleverer and gayer and wittier. No one could understand why she bothered with me. They'd written me off long ago as the permanent middle-aged bachelor who hangs round the bar reminiscing to the mess steward when everyone else has gone home to their families. Except that I wasn't in the bar. More often in the stables. It was the horses that got us together really. Rox loved to ride. She lived near the camp, and she had a horse that wasn't much good, and I had two at the time, so she used to ride my Showboat, a young one who was going to be a good jumper, and I was training them both for the hunter trials. They had a chance.' He turned round and looked at Anna, peering because he could not see her behind the lamp. 'The competition wasn't much. They could have won, but Rox got fed up and started going out with another chap in the regiment. A dark, slippery man like a snake, no one thought much of him, but he let her drink as much as she liked and stay up all night, and it made her think I was a terrible old woman because I wouldn't. This other chap thought so too. He told me once I didn't know how to treat a girl. "You fuss more about that mare

125

than about Roxie,' he said, and when she said the same thing to me the next day when she came to ride, I knew where she'd got it from. I told her she shouldn't go out with him, and she laughed and flicked me in the face and said I didn't own her. When I reminded her that she was going to marry me, I meant that she shouldn't fool around with anyone else, but she took it that marriage meant possessing, chaining, bullying. She was furious – she was so young, you see, and terribly impulsive. Beautiful. She got on Showboat and hared off on the cross-country course. They'd never done the whole thing before, and some of the jumps weren't properly made up. She came back half an hour later with a broken wrist. Showboat wasn't so lucky. She didn't come back.'

'She killed her,' Anna whispered.

'Oh no.' The Captain dropped his voice to match hers. 'It wasn't her fault. It could have happened to anyone. But Roxanne wouldn't even talk about it. She broke our engagement – it was never very tightly tied – and went away.'

He stopped and smiled at Anna, running his hand up through his hair from the back of his neck, and she asked: 'With the snake man?'

The Captain laughed abruptly, tugging at a piece of hair. 'He couldn't run anywhere. He was in the hospital. The evening after I had to shoot Showboat, I went to Roxanne's house to try to make her feel better about it. Her mother told me that she had gone out with him, plaster cast, sling and all. "You know what she is," that feeble woman said, "I can't do anything with her." I waited in the garden till they came back, and watched them go inside. When he came out, I shot him in the leg.'

'I don't blame you.'

'The Army did. You can't do that sort of thing in the Regiment. When your heart is broken, you're supposed to spray a little more starch on your moustache and order another drink. But they were pretty decent about it. I wasn't booted out. They gave me the chance to get out like a gentleman.'

'And Roxanne?'

'I've looked for her, followed up leads, but I've never found her. One day she'll come back. She'll meet someone who will
126

tell her where I am, or she'll be in this neighbourhood and hear about the Farm. She can't resist horses. She'll have to come.'

He moved to the door and flicked a switch, and the expression on his face and the bare white light from the ceiling were so matter-of-fact that Anna said quite briskly: 'She's probably married by now.'

'Perhaps. Perhaps not. I'll see her either way. See her laugh and toss her hair. Like the dead man in the sonnet, waiting.

> *'And turn, and toss your brown delightful head*
> *Amusedly, among the ancient Dead.'*

Chapter Eleven

One of the national dailies got hold of a good sob story for the porous mass of readers whom it had painstakingly conditioned in the extremes of sadism and soppiness, to match its presentation of the news.

A fifteen-year-old boy in a Black Country town, motherless since babyhood and recently orphaned by the death of his father, had been left with a hovel dwelling, a firewood round which his father had built up door-to-door over the years, a cart, a common old pony name of Bob, and a ramshackle shed to keep him in.

The boy kept the firewood business going in a half-hearted way, just enough to feed himself and pay for the dance halls and cinemas and steamy cafés where his real world began. Not enough to feed the pony. When the plucky little animal keeled over and died trying to pull a load of wood and the boy up a hill, his excuse was: 'I didn't know nothing about his food,' although he had actually helped to take care of the pony when his father was alive.

That was the truth. A reporter, doodling through a dull day in the juvenile court, picked up the story, turned it his way, which was the way of the paper who employed him, and sent it in with a photograph of the boy, a forlorn lock of hair over one eye, standing beside the empty shafts of his cart.

An orphan, struck by the cruel hand of fate. First his mother, then his father, and now the old four-legged friend who was his livelihood. 'I suppose I'll get a barrow and push the wood round,' he was credited with saying although he had never pushed anything heavier than a billiard cue and had no intention of starting now.

But the readers could not know this. They only knew what was in the paper, and they believed it as if it were the tablets of

Moses. They began to send in money, small sums, odd half-crowns from children and old ladies that could ill be spared. The newspaper reported this with quiet pride, as if they expected nothing less from their readers, and the boy was quoted as saying: 'I'll put it towards a new pony, but there'll never be another like Old Bob,' although he had in fact gone to ground in the juvenile underworld and the reporter could not find him.

More money began to come in, from those who did not want to be left out of such an appealing good deed. Some of them would not have given sixpence to a neighbour in trouble, or a recognized charity with humdrum collecting boxes. But this was different. This was a horse, and the kindly fellows at the newspaper office must not be let down.

A fair sum was subscribed, and someone – heaven knew who – went to a disreputable dealer and was talked into buying an excitable four-year-old pony for the boy. '*His Dream Come True*' ran the headline, and the charming picture of the boy and the pretty dun pony, each with a flop of forelock, was reward enough for all the widows' mites and schoolgirls' shillings.

That was it. The story was over and the readers knew no more. They did not know that the pony was wildly nervous and only half broken, completely unsuitable, and that the boy treated it so brutally that it quickly turned vicious and kicked him out of the ramshackle shed and into the hospital with a broken knee-cap, and the Captain was stuck with the dun pony.

There was room for it now at the Farm. The nurseryman's creamy Taffy had returned from a long holiday to plant his rested forelegs on the town's suburban pavements, his whiskered mouth adrool for the tributes of housewives and children. Mrs Berry's milk-white Elaine, who should never have been brought across the Irish Sea, had been mercifully unburdened of life, with Mrs Berry present in black, wearing purple eyeshadow and no lipstick.

The pony arrived in a cattle truck with a board kicked out, the floor stamped to splinters and its head rubbed raw from fighting the halter. Dora was alone in the yard when it came. The driver wanted no part of the hysterical pony, and she optimistically did not wait for help. When she backed it out, it fell sideways off the ramp, panicked, dragged the rope from her hand and was gone. She trapped it in a field, but it took Paul and the Captain and Slugger Jones half the day to corner and catch it.

The Captain had made calm, sensible horses out of nervous wrecks. He had made docile friends out of the mean ones, like Dolly. He was glad of the opportunity to salvage this young one, although he was angry at the chain of delusion and foolishness which made salvage necessary.

It reminded him of the ridiculous clamour over the Shetland pony, which was no better and no worse than a thousand Shetlands available as pets, except that they had not intruded on to domestic screens and said: I'm on the telly. Aren't I special?

'They're so conditioned by television and the newspapers telling them what their emotions ought to be that they only want what they're told to want; they're only sorry for the people they're told to be sorry for. They'll drop scalding tears over a cooked-up story like this useless boy, and shut their ears to the strangled barks of their own dog, tied to a rain barrel in the yard for years, and never let off.

'*For Years.* In this country, which foreigners jeer is too soft about pets. Chained up short, bark half gone like a man with cancer of the throat, thin as a paling fence – like Hippo's mother was when I found her dying.' He bent to pull the stubby ears of the yellow mongrel. 'Tied cowering under a lopsided dresser with her puppies shivering and starving in a drawer. And the baby in another drawer, not much better off. Oh yes, I got the baby away too, and Grandpa upstairs who should have been in hospital. Doesn't sound like me, does it? I had a holocaust that day, red glare before my eyes, and so on. I've never done anything so dashing since. Afterwards, the people who lived in that tunnel of a street were saying: We didn't know. Didn't bother would be more like it. Much easier to get a noble glow by sending five bob to a hard luck case they don't even have to check.

'And this is the result.' The dun pony with the long tangled mane was crouched up at the far end of the loose-box with his back humped and his ears laid flat. If anyone opened the door or went past quickly without a spoken warning, he almost climbed up the wall in his panic.

130

'You can get him back though,' said Dora, who believed that the Captain could do anything.

'But it should never have been necessary.' The Captain eyed the pony sadly and it eyed him back warily, the flick-knife of suspicion always ready. 'Want to help me, Dora? Want to help me teach him to believe in people again?'

'*Do I?*'

That showed. That just showed. He had got over his prejudice against girls in a stable, and look who had cured him. 'Then you do think I've been as good with the horses as a man?' She pounced eagerly, wanting him to admit it.

He laughed. 'Perhaps the horses think you are a boy with those pants and that hair.'

'Do you want to see me shovelling manure in pink satin and ringlets?'

'I like you as you are.' He patted the cropped chestnut head as if she were his favourite dog, and like his dog, Dora would have died for him.

The dun pony became Dora's project. Hers and the Captain's, but mostly Dora's, for she spent all her spare time on the nervous young pony and talked about him incessantly, boring everyone but Mrs Catchpole, who said: 'It's just her way. When a barrel is too full, you have to open the bung-hole and let some of it out.'

Dora would stand for hours just inside the stable door, holding out her hand with a titbit in it, talking steadily in a sing-song murmur, until the pony, who was too wild still to acquire a name, would at last move away from the wall a step or two towards her, neck stretched, head low, nostrils wide, ears flicking back and forth for danger.

Once just when his nose was touching Dora's motionless hand, Ron Stryker banged on the door outside and hallooed, and the pony jumped away back to the wall and stood with legs spraddled and trembling, snorting with fear.

Dora turned on Ronnie in a rage, but he laughed, leering at her over the door like a gargoyle. 'E's got to get used to noise some time. Look how they train the Police horses.'

'He's not going to be a Police horse. And if he is, I hope he tramples you in a football crowd. Look what you've done. I've spent hours getting him to come close. Now I'll have to start all over again.'

'You spend too much time with that crazy brute. Puts more work on us.'

'The Captain told me to.'

'Captain's pet.'

'I do my work! I do this in my own time.'

'Like now, I suppose,' Ron whined, 'with fifteen horses to get in out of the fields and Curly and Slugger off and just me and the old man to feed and water and bed down.'

'I didn't realize it was so late.' Dora came out of the stable, and aimed a kick at Ronnie's slickly-trousered shin. He skipped away across the yard and she ran with him and suddenly they held hands and burst into wild song. That was the odd thing about Ronnie. He could be so mean, so detestable, and then suddenly he was just young, and you could shoot up with him in an effervescent surge of energy, and laugh and laugh about nothing, as they did now, whooping and pushing and collapsing in a smother of giggles into the hay, so that Uncle, with his pitchfork threateningly close, said: 'This here is for horses to eat. How'd you like to have a horse roll on your bread and butter?'

They giggled at him like an infant school for idiots, spluttering behind their hands. With all his affected maturity, Ron could suddenly be like that, sharing the idiocy, the jumping energy of the part of sixteen-years-old that was still a child. Then suddenly he was out of it, old as the hills again, sly, lazy, suspicious. For no reason, except to spite Dora, she supposed, he decided to feed the dun pony himself, although it was her job. Instead of putting the tub of feed down just inside the door for the pony to approach in his own time, Ronnie tipped the feed noisily on to the floor and when the pony jumped, threw the zinc tub at his head.

Dora was in with Cobby two doors away. She heard the noise, saw Ron nip out of the door, saw the flung tub and the terrified pony, ran after Ron and hit him on the head.

'Fighting,' said Uncle. 'Screws loose, the pair of 'em.' But he knew what had happened in the pony's stable and he asked Dora if she was going to tell the Captain.

'I don't know.' She might have knocked Ron's teeth out if he had not jerked his head away, but she might not split on him; so Uncle went to the Captain himself.

After the Captain had talked to Ron, the boy sulked for days, and there was a lot of bitter muttering about My Uncle and This Crummy Job; but Ron was too scared either of his uncle or of the effort of finding another job to do anything but stay sullenly on at the Farm and slouch through the minimum of work.

It was dark now already at half past four, and the lights were on in the big barn where Dora and Paul were mixing the feeds in the wooden barrow. At the other end Ron was listlessly forking hay into the two-wheeled cart which they pushed around the stables to fill the racks.

'We'll be here all night, the rate you're going,' Paul called to him, as he pushed the feed barrow to the door.

'I don't feel well,' Ronnie whined. 'I'm not meself.' Paul and Dora went out and left him slumped on a bale of hay, the pitchfork between his knees like a trident, face resting slack-jawed against the handle.

Paul and Dora were half-way round with the feeds when Ronnie finally came out, tugging at the cart exhaustedly, as if it held a load of stones, not hay. They saw him throw away a cigarette end, hopping bright on the cobbles, and Paul said: 'We'll have a fire in that barn one day.'

They had a fire today. When Paul went back to the barn to get a pitchfork, a stack of bales in the corner was ablaze and the end of the barn was swirling thick with smoke. Paul sent Dora up to the house for the Captain before he got the fire extinguisher and fought with it, choking and dizzy inside the barn, to stop the fire spreading to the rest of the hay and the wooden beams and walls.

His head was swimming and it was like a dream with the Captain suddenly swimming beside him in the smoke, yelling through a red spotted handkerchief: 'Get out before you choke to death or drown!'

Drown – in a barn? Why not, if they were swimming . . . Paul dropped the heavy extinguisher and himself after it, and the Captain was dragging him fast over the dusty floor as an axe split a jagged hole and the first jet of water banged in.

Fifty tons of hay was a total loss, but the barn was saved and the stable next to it. Thanks to Paul, said the Chief Fire Officer generously, but Paul was not there to hear. He was with Uncle in his cottage across the road, with the door locked against Mrs Catchpole and Dora, because Uncle would not weep in front of women.

Because the fire might have spread to the stables on that side of the yard, the horses there had to be got out. Uncle had gone in to get his beloved Flame, but the old racehorse was panicky, pulled back and would not lead. The other horses caught her fear, so they had to be driven out, milling and slipping on the cobbles. The hay cart was pulled across the archway opening to keep them in, but old Flame, galloping stiff-legged with her eyes wild and her mouth white with the foam of terror, charged the cart, knocked it sideways, and clattered out on to the road, running faster than she had for years to meet the petrol tanker which killed her.

No one had seen Ron Stryker since Paul ran out of the barn and yelled to Dora that the hay was on fire. He did not come back to work for a week, and when he did, sauntering in with a whistle and a toss of his overgrown head, the Captain gave him his money and told him to saunter out and keep going.

Ronnie feigned amazement, but dropped it when he realized that everybody knew who had started the fire. 'It was an accident,' he whined. 'Could have happened to anybody. It wasn't my fault. No harm done anyway. My Uncle will make good the hay and that.'

'He can't make good an old racehorse,' the Captain said quietly. 'Or an old man's sorrow. Get out now, before Uncle comes. I don't want him even to see you.'

Chapter Twelve

'I read a poem once,' Phyllis said, 'where this man had a horse in the war, pulling the guns and that, and he was always crying about he wanted to see him again. Reminds you of Dad and his carry on.'

'They didn't have horses in the war,' her husband said.

'Which war?'

'Which one are you talking about?'

'How should I know?'

Phyllis and George often twisted themselves into this kind of conversational knot, from which there was no way out except to cut the string and start on something else.

So Phyllis started off again on her father. 'Him and his famous Jacky. It was only a horse, I suppose, when all's said and done. Makes you sick to see him sit dreaming there day after day like a stopped clock.'

They often talked about Tom as though he were not in the room, but he usually was, for his chest was too bad to go out in the winter and there was nowhere but the kitchen to sit in his daughter's house. She would not let him use the prim, polished front room, and his bedroom was cluttered with the guns, models, carpentry, football boots and dirty crumpled clothes of the grandson with whom he shared it. Sometimes, when the coal had come and the shed was full, there was a bicycle as well, and it was almost impossible for Tom to get in and out of bed.

Since Mother died, he had lived with his daughter in a soul-less new housing estate twenty miles from the colliery village which had held all his life. Phyllis had made a great sacrifice to take him, but she knew her duty, she hoped. She did not actually say that. She did not need to. It was in her heavy-jawed face and her clamorous nasal voice, and in the way she treated him most of the time, except when she was mellowed with beer.

After Mother's funeral, where Phyllis had stared round at the hewn, pitted mining features and the sad, strong faces of the women under the swaddling scarves, and marvelled that she might have been like that if she had not flown away, the doctor had said that Dad could not live alone. If George had objected to having him, Phyllis would have bullied the Welfare people to get him into a Home, but George, who was kinder than Phyllis in a vague way, groping towards the truths of humanity, had furrowed his oily brow into thick rolls and said: 'You owe it to the old man, I suppose, for what he did for you and Arthur.'

'Huh.' Phyllis could say it high up in her nose, like a horse. 'Pit kids. Living up to our necks in coal dust, and like to starve to death in the 1922 lock-out. Thanks for nothing.'

'How could you remember? You'd not be a year old then.'

'I remember being *born*, if you want to know.' Phyllis often used impossible statements to slap down argument.

Phyllis was the clever one. Arthur had always been the gormless one. He had worked with his father in the underground stables, forgetful, good-hearted, until he went up on the wrong side of a nervous pony in a stall and got himself kicked into next week and a job in the disabled workshop, putting the stuffing into teddy bears.

Phyllis had been to school until she was sixteen, worked in a shop for five years and married a white collar man several notches above her. Or rather above her family, for she had never considered herself on their level. She knew all the answers. Quick, she was. Her father often marvelled that he and Mother, who could read fair enough, but had never been able to write properly until the day she died, had produced such a swan. Phyllis followed the fashions and the foreign pictures, and could remember the names of film stars from years back and tell about their love lives. The old man could remember almost every one of the hundreds of ponies he had cared for underground and at the pit top, but nobody ever wanted to hear about them.

Everyone called him the old man, and he was sick and

wheezy and felt himself rotting into old age from idleness. He was only sixty-five, but the pit had taken its toll, even though he had never been a collier, but first a pony driver and then a horsekeeper and later head horseman, with five men under him and over eighty ponies in his care.

There were only fifteen ponies now at his old colliery, and would soon perhaps be none, although anyone who had worked underground knew that there were certain jobs a good pony could do better than a machine. They pulled no coal now that it was all loaded on to a moving rubber belt running parallel to the coal face. They were chiefly used to haul the tubs down the gate from the main heading, bringing pit props to shore up the roof inch by inch as the coal face advanced. The rails were laid on rough ground here and a pony was more adaptable than an engine.

When Tom was a lad, before mechanization, ponies were essential, and each man gave them the respect and affection of a colleague. Now in the few pits that still used them, they were more of a curiosity. It was hard to find boys to train as pony drivers or horsekeepers. Questions were asked on committees. The uninformed made a little play now and again with the word cruelty.

Cruelty. Tom could have told them. One reason he hated to see retired ponies given away as pets was that he knew they were not likely to get the good food and expert care they had in the pits. He had known that with Jacky, but it was not his pony, and there was nothing he could do.

Jacky, with the white onion star and the square cheeky nose that pushed and butted and lipped at you, demanding attention. Jacky, the best one he ever had. Never sick or lame a day. Game, clever, strong as a bull and gentle as a woman, liking his joke, but never too rough with it. He could pull the cork out of a tea bottle and suck it down like a baby. No one taught him that. He found it out for himself, just as he could find his way back two miles to the stables alone in the dark, if he had a mind, push open the heavy wooden door and always go right to his own stall, seventh up on the left.

Jacky, Dot, Nigger, Owen, Buller, Punch, Star, Tiger, Admiral. Tom sat in his rubbed leather chair between the kitchen

137

fire and the window, alone or with the clamour of the house about him, and told them over and over in the roll call of his memory. He remembered them all, every pony he had ever cared for. He had bought them, trained them, shod them, clipped them, fed them, doctored them, and sent them away up out of the pit when their time was done. To many of them he had brought a humane end himself, the last thing he could do for them when they were injured or sick beyond recovery.

Bobby, Ginger, Jim, Kit, Soldier, Larry lying with a broken back, still alive under the tub of coal that had tipped off the rails. Another Ginger who used to pull the clothes off your back when you were shoeing him. Sailor who lay down if you hung him on to a tub he thought was too full. John who wouldn't stand to be groomed unless you whistled Come Back to Erin. Swift little Diamond who couldn't be beat at the pony racing when the strikes were on. Pride with the coat like old silver, who won so many ribbons at the shows that the other collieries complained he was not a genuine pit pony, although he had been underground since he was four, except for strikes and holidays.

And Jacky. He was Irish bred, gleaming black like new-cut coal, and dark moleskin grey when his winter coat was clipped off. He had the fat white star and one white sock behind. When Tom's youngest grandchild, the girl they called Sandra, came to root under his bed, getting out the envelope with all the photographs, he showed her pictures of Jacky and taught her to chant: 'One white foot, keep him till the end. Two white feet, give him to a friend. Three white feet, send him far away. Four white feet, keep him not a day.'

'Four white socks is showy, Sandy, and brings the clapping, but they bring shell feet too, and don't you forget it.'

When Tom started to show Jacky, everyone else, even the flashy silver Pride, might as well have stayed home. Under the bed in the suitcase which held everything that was most dear was the bag of Jacky's ribbons and all the photographs of him at shows with Tom. Always with Tom.

Tom had bought him in a bunch of five or six others as a three-year-old and named him Jacky after a biter and bucker he had just sent back to the dealer. When he was broken, he

138

kept him a year on light work at the pit top, and he was then underground for almost sixteen years.

Tom's official explanation for keeping him down when he was over age was that he was strong and fit and might pine without his work. The private reason was that he thought – almost hoped – that he would pine without Tom.

When Tom was retired at fifty-five with a chest like a slurry dam, Jacky retired with him. He went at first to the colliery's rest home, but he was so fit and sound for his twenty years and so docile that he was given away to a family as a children's pet.

The horse-keeper at the rest home could not drive and his mate was sick, so Tom had to take Jacky in the trailer to his new home.

He would never forget it. Never forget it. As he sat by the ungenerous fire in the long, long stretches between dinner and tea, when Phyllis was gone in to the shops and the children not yet home from school, Tom tortured himself over and over, like a tongue nagging a sore tooth, with the memories he had carried for nearly ten years in some small private hell of his brain.

The gravelled drive, the newly painted house, big as a mansion, flowers neat and disciplined, like imitations. Lawns like a pool table, so unblemished you almost thought to see an embossed iron notice: KEEP OFF THE GRASS.

The garage with two fat-bottomed cars. Fancy bikes. Tennis court. Croquet. Long chairs under a striped sun-awning. A woman in some kind of garment she might have called a dress, though it looked like an indecency to Tom, coming quickly, rat-a-tat-tat down the verandah steps in shoes all heels and no toes, and making him reverse the jeep and trailer off the crescent of drive so that it would not mess the gravel.

That trailer was always a beggar to back, and Tom had left a long wheel mark on the edge of the lawn before he was headed to go round behind the garage. She carried on as if he had driven a tractor right through the garden – lawn, shrubs, tidy flower beds and all.

But when Tom saw the stable where Jacky was to go, he forgot her voice and the lawn, and everything but dismay. All that – the house, garden, tennis, cars – and this to put a horse in. *This* for a pony who had lived most of his life in colliery

139

stables that were second to none in the land. A leaning, draughty shed without even a proper half door. The door had either to be shut up tight, or just a bar across. If they left Jacky in there at night with just the bar, he'd be over it or under it and away back home like a pigeon.

But the place had been approved, and the man here was a friend of a friend of a high-up. 'We'd love to give one of your old ponies a good home. Such fun for the kids.' 'My dear chap, how charming of you. Take your pick.'

It was not Tom's pony and there was nothing he could do about it, except reflect that there were more ways of being cruel to a horse than beating it with a nailed stick.

He led Jacky sadly out of the trailer and into the shed, which had a dirt floor, gouged into holes and ruts by some other luckless horse. The woman had summoned a man in a patched jacket whom Tom took to be the gardener, but who turned out to be her husband, and he told Tom: 'Better tie him up till we see how quiet he is.'

'You couldn't want a quieter.' Tom was slipping off the halter, but: 'Tie him up, I said,' snapped the man in the patched jacket, so he shrugged his shoulders and knotted the halter rope through a ring in the rough wooden manger.

'He won't like it,' Tom said. 'He wants tying with a neck collar, same as he's always had.'

'Well, he's not in the pit now,' the man said briskly. 'He'll get used to it.'

As Tom came out of the shed, Jacky pulled back, braced himself, and broke the halter.

'Get the bar up!' the man yelled, and Tom had to laugh, wretched as he was.

'He's not a wild beast.' He took his time about pushing the pony gently back and slipping the bar across. 'They told me he were to be in a meadow,' he muttered, hearing himself surly, unable to better it. 'He's earned his time at grass, you know.'

The man flushed, and looked almost guilty. 'He will be,' he said quickly. 'I want the kids to see him as soon as they get home. He – he's for them.'

The children came back from school before Tom left, and he saw why their father had sounded almost ashamed of wanting to please them. They ignored his greeting entirely, as if he were no more than a shrub by the driveway. Running to the shed, they stopped short a few yards from Jacky's nose, so that he had to stretch his neck out over the bar like a giraffe begging for peanuts.

They seemed nervous of him, like the parents. What did they want a pony for then if they were afraid of it? If the father was looking to get favour from his children, why didn't he buy a pony instead of taking a free one who had worked all his life for something better than this?

The children still paid no attention to their father, but the girl, who did not look too bad, came running up to Tom as he was climbing into the jeep, unable to take his leave of Jacky, or even look at him, and said quite winsomely: 'Thank you for bringing us our pony.'

Our Pony! Tom nodded and smiled with his Little Missy face, but could not answer.

Sitting in the leather chair, with the room growing dark and the dull street outside in twilight, though it would jump into blackness as soon as Phyllis banged in and switched on the light, Tom could still feel his hands on the wheel, see ahead through the muddy glass, as he drove home with the empty trailer bouncing behind him, and his heart a leaden weight.

He went back once to see Jacky, and found him in a meadow. Shade, water, good sweet grass. Had he been tormenting himself for nothing? Jacky knew him, of course, but when the sugar and carrots were gone, he moved away, grazing contentedly.

Soon after that, Tom was very ill and had to go into hospital. When he went to see Jacky, months later, the people had gone. The house was empty, with Sale boards up. Tom asked at the house across the road: 'Did they take the pony?'

'To London?' The woman laughed. 'I believe they gave it away. They offered it to us, but it was too old. We didn't want it. Nippy thing.'

Nippy? So it had been as bad as he feared. Jacky had never nipped. Take your hat off, get you in the seat of the pants when you had his back foot between your knees, putting him a shoe on. Never nip. What had they done to him?

'But wait.' The woman had called him back up her brick path which gaped and heaved as if she had laid it herself, without sand. 'If you're really looking – I remember them saying – a builder, was it?' She beat the side of her head lightly with clenched knuckles. 'I remember they took him away tied to the tailboard of a little truck.'

'They'd ought to give him back to the colliery,' Tom told her, as he had before.

'That's not my fault.' The woman retreated into her doorway like a snail. 'I'm only trying to help. I'm only telling you.'

He had to go then, to catch the bus. He had come back later, and again another day, to ask at some builders' yards, but it had been difficult to make them understand, since they had no pit pony, nor ever had, nor any intention of having one.

Then he was ill again, and the months went by in feebleness, and the years, and then Mother, who had spent a lifetime on her feet, was suddenly in bed, and then she died. The doctor said he could not be alone, so he moved in with George and Phyllis, away from the black hillside village that had been his life, away from the wheels and derricks and pit heaps that had been his landscape, away to the prim, flat housing estate outside the small town where George was an auctioneer's clerk.

As he sat in the kitchen there four years later, parading all his sturdy ponies through his waking dreams, he thought a lot about Jacky, and what it would be like to see him again. That time he had been back and found him in the meadow, he had known him at once. Hadn't he come right to the gate, and when Tom closed his hand on the sugar, curved his neck and lifted his right knee in the old way?

He would know him still. But he'd be thirty now. He was likely dead. As he sat by the close-fisted coke fire whose draught doors Phyllis was always clanging shut to make it burn more slowly, Tom grieved himself with all the bad things that could have happened to Jacky. He thought of him dying in agony somewhere alone. Being destroyed and Tom not there to hold his head. Crumpling down in the knacker's yard . . .

'I reckon he's still alive,' he remarked at tea, and everyone

142

pounced on him. Phyllis, the boy, little Sandy, who did not always take his part, the elder girl, named Darlene after some film star who had been.all the go when she was born.

George did not pounce. He sighed heavily, as he often did, though he was not a sad man, and said, crumbing cake: 'I read about a goat lived to be fifty.'

'This was a *horse*.' His wife dragged out the word like a bray.

'No, a goat. I saw the picture in the paper.'

'What paper?'

'The one I saw it in. Fifty years old.'

'You're daft. A horse couldn't be fifty years old.'

'I'm talking about a goat.'

Darlene got up abruptly with a shriek of her chair and flounced out, banging the door, and they heard her gramophone blast into bedevilled song. She did this half-way through almost every meal, unless the pudding was worth staying for. It indicated that she was through with the family, driven to the breaking point. Tom remembered Phyllis doing the same thing years ago, only without the gramophone.

'I'd ought to followed it up,' he continued as if the pouncing and the argument and the flouncing had not interrupted him, 'after Mother died. But I hadn't the strength.'

'Well, you certainly wouldn't have the strength now,' Phyllis informed him. 'Your chest is like a sewer.'

'If I'd gone back and asked around again, someone would have known something about that pony.' Tom went on, not listening to her. She talked about his chest viciously, as if it were separate from himself, a criminal.

That Sunday, with a pale sun parting at last the drizzling pall that had hung about the bare countryside for days, George came sheepishly to the old man. 'Want to go for a drive, Dad?'

'Don't bother to ask if I want to go,' Phyllis said, not expecting to hear the answer: 'I wasn't going to. We may stop off at some of the pubs.'

To get her own back, Phyllis held them up a long time fussing, pouring gargles down her father's throat, bundling him up with woollens, mufflers, gloves, running out just when they were off at last with a blanket for his knees.

'She's a good woman.' When they were out of sight, Tom began to unwind himself from the suffocating tokens of his daughter's pique. 'Where to, George?'

George was embarrassed. He changed gear with a noise of gnashing teeth, hooted at a chicken, fumbled in his jacket for a cigarette. 'I thought –' He lit the cigarette, coughed, threw the match out of the window, stuck the already wet end of the cigarette between his lips and mumbled through it. 'I thought you might like to go back and see if you could find out what happened to that pony.'

'You're much too kind, lad.' The old man felt himself grow feeble. You would think that sudden kindness would give you strength, but it weakened you, if you were not expecting it. 'You don't have to do that for me.'

'No.' George sighed. 'But it just hit me that we don't seem to do very much for you. The pony is dead, I suppose, but at least you'd know. You'd have the truth in your mind. It would be like – like laying a ghost, see? You'd not have that *turmoil*.' He brought out the unaccustomed word deliberately, furrowing his brow and leaning forward to savage his innocent cigarette in the ashtray. 'My own Dad died at sea, as you know, and he and I had never made up our quarrel. I'd like . . . I'd like . . .' He scratched his forehead, pushing his sporty week-end cap to the back of his head.

He drove seriously, observing all the rules, sitting up very straight with his arms braced out, as if he were driving a bus. Tom, who hardly ever went out in a car, rode like a king, giving the nod to all the familiar landmarks coming by. The pit heaps in the distance beyond the chimneys and slanted roofs of the pipe works, the canal bridge, the sports ground where they had the pony races before someone at the Coal Board dreamed up the idea that it was cruel, the turn off to the old village itself, where Arthur and Phyllis had played and fought and sprouted out of their clothes more happily than she now seemed to remember.

'Direct me,' George said, and Tom directed him, remembering every turn, every hill, every scatter of houses on the road he had driven with Jacky, and driven back half silly from grief with the empty trailer rattling behind.

'That old horse in the little field by himself,' Corinne said, with her cherry red pout, and a shake of the long yellow pony-tail she secretly believed that Dora secretly envied, 'I think it's dying.'

Dora raced round to the little enclosure beyond the foaling stable, but Charley was only lying down, as he often did when the sun was out. He was flat on his side with his neck stretched out and his hips and ribs sticking up like coathangers, but there was nothing wrong with him.

When Dora went into the paddock and knelt down by him, he raised his bearded head and mumbled on her hand with his loose old teeth and slobbery lips, then closed his eyes and re-laxed again, breathing in short contented grunts.

'I thought he was dead.' Corinne sat down in the dark winter grass and put her large grubby hand on Charley's foot. 'How do they die – I mean when they die? I've never seen a dead horse.'

'Sometimes you just go to the stable one morning and they've had it,' Dora said. 'Like people. He died quietly in his sleep, they say when it's people, and I hope it's like that with horses. With the old codgers here, it's usually obvious when they're ready to go, and the vet comes with the humane killer. They just sort of sag, that's all. They don't feel a thing.'

'You mean you've actually *seen* a horse killed?' Corinne had an unattractive habit of tilting her moon face round and staring into yours very close, without blinking.

'Why not? They must have someone with them they know.'

'Oh, I couldn't.' Corinne shuddered all through her big frame and got up from the grass. 'I just know I couldn't.'

'You might have to,' Dora stood up and slapped at her knees, spreading the mud further. 'If there was no one else.'

'Not me. I'm too sensitive.' Corinne was still saying things like that, although everyone at the Farm had got her number within a few days of her arrival. 'I couldn't bear to see a creature hurt.'

Dora did not bother to repeat that the horse felt nothing. Corinne was a good-hearted girl, and did her work. The slop she passed out among the inmates of the Farm: 'Isn't he simply sweet?' and: 'Oh, the poor darling pet!' was harmless enough, as long as you kept her away from the Captain. And it was certainly an improvement on the possibility of sly cruelties which no one had ever actually been able to pin on to Ron Stryker.

Although the Captain had sworn that he would not have another girl in the stable, he had not been able to find a man or boy to replace Ronnie. While they were still short-handed, Dora's mother had come one Sunday to find out why she had not been home for more than a month.

She assessed the situation with her usual unarguable logic, brushing aside Dora's honest explanation that she had been working extra hours. Having tea in the farmhouse kitchen, for Tiny had a big thing about people's mothers and would not turn one away unfed, she had seen Paul, in a red and white sweater, with his black hair rumpled and his face flushed from working in the cold. She had confided to Tiny at the sink, where she always dutifully migrated as a guest, whether her hostess wanted her to or not, that she did not think it right for Dora to be the only girl here.

'There's me,' Tiny said, dashing hot water into an upturned spoon, and soaking both their feet.

The mother raised an eyebrow to imply: Fat lot of good that is, and said: 'I mean in the stables. That boy –'

'My Paul? Don't let me hear a word against my Paul.' Tiny reacted instantly, puffing herself up like a startled toad. 'Poor motherless fellow. First time he's had a proper family. He's like my own, I'll tell you that, if you can understand it –' Tiny could be just as civilly insulting as Dora's mother – 'and Dora is like his sister.'

'I'm glad you think so.' Dora's mother polished deliberately, round and round the coloured border of a plate. 'I value freedom as much as anyone else, I suppose. I've let Dora have her way in this absurd job because it was her choice, but I think she should come away now and start some kind of worth-while, more feminine career.'

Tiny laughed. 'Can you see her?' not believing that she meant it, thinking that it was just idle sink talk, like she and Slugger indulged in sometimes when the dishes had piled up all

146

day, playing that they were rich and famous. But the mother went to the Captain and announced that Dora could not stay in a job where she was the only girl.

'Well, I can't lose you,' the Captain told Dora, and she wondered if he guessed at even one thousandth part of the splendour of his words. 'You'll have to go into town to the employment office and see if you can find a girl who knows the front end of a horse from the back.'

So Dora had found Corinne, large, buxom, harmless, silly, willing, amiable and strong. At first she irritated the others, like a puppy underfoot, but she was so well-meaning that she was vulnerable, like a puppy, and the irritation had mellowed to the tolerance given to a puppy.

Mrs Catchpole had been tolerant of her all along, as she was with everybody. She had her in her other attic bedroom, opposite Dora, and gave patient ear to the ingenuous prattle and the recital of personal preferences in food, colours, Christian names, flowers and pop singers, which was Corinne's idea of conversation.

But she was genuinely fond of horses, under the sugar icing of endearments, and she worried over them as if they were premature infants. She worried about the Cobbler's good eye, which was becoming more cloudy, although he was still pulling the blue cart cheerfully, without stumbling, and could discern obstacles even on his blind side, with the extra sense of presence that enables a sightless man to avoid the furniture in an unfamiliar room.

Corinne infuriated Paul by harping on how terrible it would be when he was totally blind. 'To think he will never jump again,' she would sorrow, with her silly forlorn face on. 'The poor beautiful thing. I wonder if he knows. I wonder if he minds dreadfully . . .'

She was very worried about Charley. 'Uncle says you're going to have the pit pony put to sleep,' she told the Captain. 'Is it true?'

'I don't know. He seems to be all right.'

'You know he's not,' said Uncle, sniffing his underlip up into his nose. 'Come on man, what's the matter with you? You've put down horses not near as far gone as that one.'

'Oh don't,' Corinne said, and would have gripped his arm with heavy pleading hands, but he twitched her off. 'Don't persuade him. Charley is so sweet, and when you think of all those years and years underground, working in slavery to keep people like us warm – I couldn't bear him to die. Let him see the spring, and the new grass.'

''E can't eat, the beggar,' Uncle said.

'I can't bear it.' Corinne's easily filled eyes swam with tears, and the Captain, who would normally be nauseated by the display, surprisingly said: 'Let's give him a while longer then,' as if using the excuse of her to settle his own doubt.

When Uncle began to nag him again later, the Captain said: 'But if Charley goes, you won't have anything to show to visitors as the oldest horse in the world.'

'I'll show that walking bed frame of Mrs Berry's,' said Uncle, who could not bring himself to call the skewbald Guinevere. 'Looks twice its age. No problem in that.'

'I've seen you before,' said the woman with the tilting red brick path, when she opened the door and found Tom and George on her doorstep, caps in hand. 'Let's see now – wherever –' She knuckled her brains with the same gesture as before, although she had changed with the years, shrunk a little, and her hair was quite white.

When Tom reminded her, she said at once: 'Oh, I am glad to see you!' and made them come in out of the cold. Not to sit down in a room, but at least into the hall, which was an improvement on last time.

'I led you astray,' she said, 'and I've never forgiven myself. A builder, I told you, and you hadn't been gone over an hour before I remembered it was a plumber. I could see how much you wanted to find the pony, and when the people had him across the road, they told me that the man who brought him from the colliery had been so upset that he nearly took off their gatepost when he drove out, so I guessed that was you.'

Leaning against the coatstand, because his legs would not hold him firm for very long, Tom nodded and looked down. He did not like to think of those people who had taught Jacky to nip discussing his distress with her. Laughing about him. Joking about sueing the Coal Board for the scratches on the paint.

'I've felt so bad ever since then.' The woman clasped her hands. 'You'll never believe this,' She looked from Tom to George, challenging them, 'but sometimes I've even prayed to the Good Man that you would come back.'

This embarrassed George into a show of spirit. He shuffled his feet and said: 'It would have made more sense to get hold of the colliery manager and ask Dad's name.'

But praying to the Good Man was less trouble. 'It's always easy to be wise after the event,' she said less warmly. 'But I'll tell you something that *will* surprise you. I not only remembered that the pony had gone to a plumber, but I remembered the name I saw painted on the little van. It wasn't a local firm, no one I knew, and I kept the name by me, because it was so odd. Seth Stillwater and Sons. Isn't that a fine name for a plumber? So I've had that bit of useless information all these years. And now it isn't useless any more, although that pony was quite old when he was here, and must be dead by now, I suppose.'

The more people kept saying that Jacky was dead, the more stubbornly Tom believed that he was alive. He would be only thirty now. If he had had a good home . . . if he'd been properly cared for . . .

Seth Stillwater was dead, and one of his sons had moved out, but they found the other one, still plumbing, in a village six miles away. He was out thawing pipes, but his wife was at home with a farrow of fat children with bursting red veins on their cheeks, and when she saw that Tom was cold and tired, she brought him and George in to sit by the fire, and made them a cup of tea.

When she stopped bustling and they could pin her down about Jacky, her first remark was: 'Ah, the poor thing. I did feel badly.'

In spite of the tea and the fire and the steaming fug of the room full of people and children, Tom was suddenly as cold as death. When he reached out to put down his teacup, the cup clattered in the saucer like bones. So it had been here that it had happened. Out there in the nice little tarred stable, or perhaps in the orchard where there were now two other ponies grazing.

'How did he —' His cough shook and enfeebled him. 'How — how did he die?' he managed to whisper at last.

'Die? Bless you,' said the woman cheerily, coming over to pat him on the back, although it was obviously not that kind of cough. 'Who said he died? Fit as a flea, he was when he went, and going strong now for all I know, the rascal.'

When the cough reawakened by her slaps on the back had subsided, one of the elder boys, working with a clamp and handsaw in the corner, called across the room to Tom: 'Blackie got out through the fence one night and gone off, no halter on, nor nothing.'

He bent again to his woodwork, and the mother went on: 'We couldn't find him and we couldn't find him, and we'd been so fond of him — young Ted there was only a baby at the time, but his elder brother used to ride Blackie and thought the world of him — and so after a bit we put a piece in the paper, and a man stopped by from Deerfield, right over the other side of the hills, and said he'd got him at his place.'

Deerfield, at least ten miles from here. The other side of the hills. So he'd been on his way back to the pit. Back to Tom.

'You get him back?' George asked, and the mother shook her head. 'We wanted to, for we all set store by that little monkey, but the man told us his tale, and —' she shrugged her fatly padded shoulders and smiled benevolently — 'there was nothing we could do about it.'

'You see —' A girl about fourteen was standing by Tom's chair, smiling down at him through a curtain of fair silky hair. 'His little boy was very ill, something with his heart. He laid in bed all the time in a room downstairs by the window, and one morning early when he had awoke, he turned his head to see the birds, and seen our Blackie on the lawn outside, eating grass. When his mother came in to him, she found the little boy tapping a peppermint on the window, and Blackie bumping up with his nose against the glass outside. They knew they'd be right to tell the Police, but the boy begged for Blackie, and so they set up some hurdles on the lawn and kept him there, where he could see him.'

150

'We went over to him once,' the mother said. 'It was summer, and the window open, and there was that old pony stood with his nose on the window-ledge asleep and the child in his bed asleep too, with his little bird's hand out on the sill.'

The Weaver had colic. 'And serve him right,' the Captain said: 'I'm surprised he's not had it before.'

The disgusting gulps of air which the Weaver loved to suck in, hanging with his long teeth on to the edge of any convenient object, had backed up on him at last, and he was a sorry horse.

When Corinne went in to feed him, she came out screaming like a jay. She was dreadful in a crisis. It was a mercy she had not been there when the barn caught fire.

The old Police horse was standing with his legs splayed out and his head down almost to the ground, his forehead jammed against the wall. He weaved his gas-filled body back and forth, and from time to time, he would shake his head violently, then turn round to looked balefully at his flatulence, groan, and jam his aching brain up against the wall again.

'He's having a fit!' Corinne screamed, but Paul got a halter and a pair of thick gloves, for the horse was tormented enough to grab at anything, put the halter on him and dragged him outside to walk him round the yard.

'Keep 'em moving,' he told Corinne. 'Try and break up the wind. If you let 'em be, they'll get a strangulated gut and then you've had it.'

'I thought he'd gone mad. But he looks all right now,' Corinne said wonderingly. She put out a hand, but the Weaver laid back his ears and drew his nostrils away from his teeth. 'I know just how he feels,' she said. 'When I came round after my appendix, I bit the nurse who was holding the basin.'

After the vet had come to give the Weaver a colic drench, he went round to the foaling stable to look at Charley, who was mumbling and dribbling his soft feed. 'And that isn't doing him much good by the looks of him,' he told the Captain. 'Why don't you give the old fellow a break?'

'I asked you round to give a drench. You never come here without wanting to kill something.'

'Tomorrow?' The vet was walking to his car, hands in pockets, kicking at pebbles with a swing of his sharply flared breeches.

'I'll be in town all day.'

Knowing the Captain, the vet did not ask what difference that made. He said: 'Day after.'

'That's Sunday.'

'Monday then. I have to come this way.'

'I'm going to London.'

'When will you be back?'

'Thursday.'

'All right. I'll be over Friday.'

'Well, look –'

'You want me to report you?' the vet asked, and it was hard to tell if he was joking because he did not smile when he joked.

'All right,' the Captain said at last. 'Friday.'

Because they planned to go out again next Sunday, and every Sunday after that until they reached the end of the trail, Tom and George told Phyllis that they had met the doctor while they were out, and he had said that her father should get out in the car as much as possible.

'Good, I'll come with you.'

'Look dear –' George kept his newspaper up, since he was not experienced in lying to his wife. 'You'd have to sit at the back, because Dad can't be near the exhaust, and you might take a cold. We're to have the windows open, so he can get a real blow.'

'Get a blow,' she said. 'You'll kill him. What are you trying to do? He's got nothing to leave, you know.' Sharply, with the voice she used for talking about death and legacies.

'Don't you know they put T.B. patients up on the mountainside with all the windows open?' George was inspired to say loftily. Last Sunday's adventure had roused his blood for the chase, and he was just as set on finding the pony as Tom was.

'Dad hasn't got T.B.,' Phyllis grumbled. 'Blow or not blow, that's the first time I've ever heard you worry about my health, and if you two go out next Sunday, I'm coming along to see what you get up to.'

152

She was very suspicious all week, and would have forced herself into the car on Sunday, but her cousins arrived unexpectedly with three large booted boys to spend the day. Tom's luck was holding. He took it as a good omen that they would find Jacky.

He sang a little, hoarsely, as they drove along like liberated prisoners, with all the windows tightly closed. When they reached the small town of Deerfield, he navigated Tom by the map the plumber's wife had drawn. A square white house with a slate roof, she had said, and there it was, creeperless and blank, with a blind blue front door and no hint of the lives within.

George stopped the car just before the gate, so that they could see the lawn behind the house. There were no hurdles there. No pony.

'It's nippy,' Tom said, although it was much warmer today. 'He'll be under cover.'

'It might be the wrong house,' George said.

It was the right house. A man with a loose, lined face told them that his son had died six months after the pony came. Erebus, he had called him, because he had come to him out of the night. The man had wanted to keep him, since the boy had loved him so, but his wife could scarcely bear to see him, for the same reason.

He was too old to sell. Too charmed to destroy. They had given him to an old lady who took in everything on four legs, but was indifferent to the needs of those who went on two. She quarrelled with the man who looked after Erebus, and he left her with the pony and the goats and the asthmatic cow. She gave the pony to her grandchildren, twenty miles away, and they rechristened him Charley, and taught him to climb the stairs.

'She'll kiss us for this,' George said, as he turned the car outside the lifeless white house and headed it away from home; but they dared not leave it until next Sunday. The luck of the dice did not throw up cousins every time. It was quite late when they got home, and Phyllis was in a snorting rage.

'Don't ask me for supper,' she cried from the kitchen, before they had even got their coats off. 'Just don't ask me, that's all I say.'

If that were really all, they would be lucky.

'John and Ethel gone then?' George asked innocently, lingering in the hall.

'I should hope so. They stayed long past their time to see you – why, I don't know – and they took it as a deliberate insult that you didn't come back. We'll not see *them* again in a hurry.'

'Good,' said George, ungratefully, for if the cousins were to drop down dead tomorrow, they had fulfilled their purpose in life today.

Tom had scarcely heard his daughter's aggrieved voice. He tottered into the kitchen beaming, fell into his chair, for he was very tired, and crowed at her: 'We done it!'

'Done what? We've done it, he says, coming home at all hours. Done what?' She stood over him with her arms akimbo, belabouring him with her voice like one of those colliery wives she had never wanted to be, scolding a drunken husband.

The child Sandra came in to see what the row was, although a row was not a curiosity in that house, and her grandfather pulled her to his knee and said breathlessly: 'I've found Jacky.'

'He's out of his mind,' said Phyllis more placidly.

At the fall of her voice, George put his head round the door and then moved his thickset body in after it with a hopeful: 'Hullo all.'

The three women, his wife, his youngest child, and his teenage daughter, biting the quicks of her nails over a magazine, looked at him without emotion. Not with antipathy or scorn. Just with nothing.

'Not exactly *found* him, eh Dad?' Rubbing his hands, he came over to the fire with the tentative, tiptoeing walk he used when he was not sure of his reception.

'As good as.' Tom spoke to Sandra, whose wandering interest was now half captured. 'He's at a farm where they take old horses. Quite a way off, up in the hills somewhere in the next county.'

'Is he still alive?' Sandy twisted his waistcoat button.

154

'If he's at that place, he will be.' Tom stared into her blank young eyes and felt his own begin to water treacherously. 'Old Jack – he's only thirty. That's nothing in a place like that, where they know how to favour them. We're going there next week, your Dad and I. Want to come, love?'

Sandy said: 'I'll see,' not realizing the honour of the invitation.

'And what,' asked Phyllis, livid at not being invited too, although she would not now have gone if you paid her, 'if I may be so bold to ask, do you propose to do with this animal, in the unlikely event you do find him? Bring him here, no doubt, and move out my runner beans and washing line to accommodate him.'

'I just want to see him, Phyll, that's all,' Tom said reasonably. That was all he did want. He wanted to see him, get him fixed in his mind's eye, have a picture of him as he was now to set beside the many memories of him in his prime.

'See his grave, more like,' said Phyllis, 'or a tin of dog meat with his name on the label.'

'Shut up with that,' George said surprisingly, and his elder daughter raised her sulky eyes momentarily from the magazine. 'We're going anyway, like it or not, and I'll not have you belittle.'

The old man turned to give him a grateful nod, but George had already left the room. When he did work up enough firing power to talk back, it was hit and run.

'It's Friday,' Uncle said at noon. 'I thought the vet was coming over to Charley.'

'His wife telephoned this morning. He's in bed with bronchitis.' The Captain smiled complacently, and no more was said.

Nothing was said on Saturday, and nothing on Sunday, and then Dora, coming across the road from the cottage in the afternoon to work with her wayward three-year-old, found the two men wandering uncertainly through the archway that led to the stable yard.

There were few visitors in winter, and usually none on a day like this, with a raw wind from across the valley blowing smack into the Farm through the leafless trees.

'Hullo,' she said, and the men turned guiltily, as if she had caught them trespassing. The younger one snatched off his cap, and the frail, older one grinned at her with an old-fashioned but serviceable set of teeth.

She walked with them into the yard. She liked old men with faded blue eyes and clean white hair. 'You want to see the horses?'

'Just one.' The old man put his hand on her arm and turned her to him so that he could see the truth in her face before she answered. 'Just Jacky.'

She frowned and shook her cropped head. 'There's no –' she began, but seeing the tension in his sick, furrowed face, she made it less harsh with: 'Perhaps he was here before me. I haven't been here very long.'

'Then it's too late.' The old man who was neither tall nor substantial, seemed to shrink further into himself, like a dying leaf.

The younger one, who had been standing uncertainly by with his mouth hanging open, as if the old man and Dora were talking a foreign language, suddenly came to his wits.

'It's the wrong name, Dad. They called him something else. You know that. Blackie, they said.'

'Erebus.' The old man looked at Dora like a hopeful child. 'Erebus, he called him, because he come out of the night.'

'No,' said the other. 'At the last it was – what was it? Billy ... Jimmy ... Dicky ... Johnny ...'

He came out with Charley at the same time as the old man said proudly, but in a whisper, because he had been coughing: 'He's a pit pony,' and Dora jumped out of her low-slung shoes with a squeak of delight.

Charley was lying down, as he often did in the afternoons, sometimes not getting up at feed time, so that someone had to squat by him with a tub of mash. Dora let the old man go alone up to the door of the loose-box, and the younger man hung back with her nervously, as if there might be a ghost in the stable. In silence, they watched the old man look over the door, and watched him fumble with the bolt, open it and go inside, moving like a sleepwalker.

'Why didn't you go in with him?' Corinne asked afterwards, thrusting her ingenuously inquisitive face close. 'Oh, it must have been sweet. I'd have given anything to be there. If you'd had a camera, you could have taken a picture of them together and called it Old Pals.'

'I went to fetch the Captain,' Dora said shortly. Useless to try to explain to Corinne that Charley and the old man had to be alone.

'I know,' said Corinne, 'because I was in the office using the typewriter to write a formal letter to that boy I can't stand any more. When Tiny called out to him that an old miner had come to see Charley, what do you think he said?'

'What?' Dora backed away a little.

'He was over at the shelves, looking something up in a book, and he just said: "I know." Quite quietly like that, without even looking up. "I know," he said and shut the book up with a sigh, smiling to himself.'

'He couldn't have known.'

'He's psychic,' Corinne said mysteriously. 'He's got what they call E.S.P.'

'What does that stand for?'

'I don't know, but he's got it.' Corinne was mildly in love with the Captain too.

Tom stayed in the stable with Charley for a long time. George hung about, looking at his watch, clearing his throat, pacing nervously, dropping hints about how far they were from home. The old man was telling the Captain the saga of Charley's greatness. He had brought all his rosettes in a brown paper bag, and was not to be stopped until the last ribbon had been accounted for, the last anecdote retold.

Did Charley remember him? Ronnie would have scoffed that he was always pleased to see anybody who came into his stable, especially if their pockets were stuffed with sugar.

Corinne was not there, fortunately, to cry: 'Oh, he knows him! Look, he's trying to say he's glad in his own funny way. If only he could speak!'

But the Captain saw, and Dora saw, that there was something in the stable that could not be expressed in words. Charley

157

looked the same – grizzled, sagging, bearded, with a blurred blue eye and a loose wet jaw. And yet there was an unmistakable difference, a rallying of the spirit, as if Tom's voice and touch awoke in him as many memories as the sight and feel of him brought surging back to Tom.

Chapter Thirteen

A week later, the pit pony was found dead in his stable, stretched out flat in the straw, as he had so often lain asleep and shamming dead, with his ribs collapsed liked a pricked balloon.

'As if he had just waited to see his old friend,' Corinne wept, and everybody rounded on her for saying what they privately thought themselves.

'But it was fate,' she said. 'The Captain putting off the end time and again – just as if he *knew*. If the old fellow had come and found Charley gone . . . but something stayed the Captain's hand. He's psychic, that's what it is.'

'Oh, dry up,' said the Captain, who was a little unnerved by the unexpected vindication of his stubbornness over Charley. 'I don't like to take life away from an animal until he's quite finished with it, that's all.'

'Then why did you say in the office: "I know," when Tiny shouted to you that the miner had come?'

'I didn't.' He had not been able to explain these two uncalculated words, even to himself.

'You did, for I was there and heard you. "I know," you said, and shut the book as if you had come to the end of the story.'

'Well – I must have meant that I – that you just have to know with animals when it's their time to go. You have to be quite sure, or you couldn't play God and condemn them. I just wasn't sure yet about Charley. I don't know why.'

'*I* know why,' Corinne said with satisfaction. 'It's because you're psychic.'

'The Captain is psychic,' she told Anna when she met her at the stables on her weekly visit to Wonderboy before she went in to the office. She told it to Callie, dreamily combing Hero's thin mane while the circus horse slept, with his eyes closed and his lower lip hanging. She told it to the vet when he came with the remains of his bronchial cough and found that Charley had jumped the gun.

She told it to the visitors, when they began to come trickling in again at week-ends as the spring crept grudgingly forward. 'The Captain is psychic,' she informed them, and they would stare at him as if he were a freak horse and drop an extra sixpence in the red and white collecting box.

With the coming of spring and the gradual softening of the winds and rains, the Night Riders began to emerge sporadically from wherever they had been holed up for the winter.

A few local boys were caught, clumsily aping the lunatic craze, but the real cunning and cruelty came from the town. On a Saturday night, gangs of boys would come out looking for excitement when the dance halls and cinemas and cafés shut down. Many of them had scooters and motorcycles or ramshackle cars and old taxis they had resurrected from the scrap yards. Since their favourite hunting grounds nearer town were being watched, and the horse owners more careful, they were maurauding further afield.

A dairyman lost a piebald cob for two days and found him trapped in wire, badly cut and lamed. A mare in foal from a village in the hills behind the Farm was ridden half to death in the park of the deserted Manor, and found in the swampy ground at the end of the lake, with her foal dead beside her.

At week-ends, and especially when the moon was full, some of the men began to keep watch again, and the Captain would often go out in the middle of the night to check his stables. Tiny knew, because the mongrel mother who slept with her heaving puppies in a box by her bed would hear him and Hippo prowling, and sit up in the box, whining and tense.

Sometimes he and Paul would go out with the other men, or scouting on their own, and it was often Paul's idea. They were both concerned about the horses, but Paul had another and a deadly serious intent, and Dora knew that he would use the revolver, if he had to.

'Why can't I come?' she kept asking.

'Because you're a girl.'

'I'm as strong as you ... Almost,' she amended, rubbing her

upper arms after a brief struggle. 'I do a man's work in the stable. The Captain says –'

'The Captain says you can't come. We don't want you.'

'You go round the pubs, I suppose. That's why you never catch anybody.'

'We will. We'll catch the Hyena one of these days. It was one of his lot they caught with that cart mare down by the gravel pits. I'm sure he's mixed up in this.'

'Then what will you do?'

'Fight to the death,' Paul said grimly, and the light leaped in Dora's eyes as she begged: 'Oh, let me come!'

On Easter Saturday, when the Captain had taken Anna to the theatre, the moon came up high and full, and laid the land below the hill in silver. Dora was in her bedroom when Paul whistled outside. She opened her window and saw him in his white sweater like a statue in Uncle's potato patch, his shadow drawn in carbon.

'Someone just telephoned to say they'd heard a horse go by on the road the other side of the racecourse. They thought it might be one of ours. It isn't, but I'm going to see what's up. Want to come?'

'I thought you said –' Dora was dying to go, but not if it was a favour. He had to want her.

'Never mind what I said. If they've gone up by the Manor, where they took that mare, it'll need at least two of us.'

'Ought we to take Slugger or Uncle?' She did not suggest Corinne.

'Take all night to get em going. More fun just you and I, anyway. Come on, kid.'

They took the little fifteen-hundredweight truck from its nook between bales of straw and bags of lime and grass seed, and Paul drove fast along the switchback road at the top of the hills, past the big field where the horse-boxes were parked for the races, and the wooden sentry box askew by the gate where they took the money for the cars.

The Manor stood apart from the village, long since abandoned, desolate, unsaleable, crumbling spookily into decay. The ugly stone house, patched and stained with the weather, stood bleakly on a rise of ground in its own parkland. Stark in the

161

moonlight, it looked down the pitted, weedgrown drive to the road with blind eyes long since deserted by the soul, its twin turrets like petrified ears at each corner, the broken balustrade of the terrace a grim skull mouth of rotting teeth.

Paul stopped the truck on the side of the road before they got to the gate, and they rang along the grass verge under the rusted iron fence which still ran all round the park with trees growing unconcernedly up through it, and bushes and twining creepers camouflaging its ugly twisted spikes.

'I hate this place.' When they came to the crenellated lodge, with all its windows broken and a chimney fallen across the porch, Dora looked up the drive at the cold dead house and shuddered.

Ahead of her, Paul was in the gateway, casting about like a foxhound. 'Look!' he said excitedly. 'They did come in here.'

Since the park was used for grazing cows and sheep, the heavy iron gates were kept open, and hurdles put across to keep the cattle in. The hurdles were down now, and there were hoof-marks and the furrows of wheels in the soft gravel; oil patches, cigarette ends, trodden turf where a horse had trampled.

The park stretched wide away from them on either side, rough, partly wooded, the lower end hidden behind the shoulder of a hill.

'No use looking for them,' Paul said in the tense, tight-lipped voice of adventure. 'If they're in here, we've got em. There's only two ways out – this gate and the back one, and they'd have to cross the bridge to get to that. I'll stay here. You go on up to the house and watch the bridge. If you see anything, hoot like an owl.'

'That wouldn't deceive anyone.'

'I don't care. It'll bring me.'

'I'd rather stay here.' The lodge was scary, with its suggestion of witches, and children being lured inside and coming out not looking like children; but the road was here, even if it was empty under the flooding moon, and the truck was here, even if she could not drive it. 'You go to the house and I'll stay here.'

'No. They'd probably come out this way.'

'What would you do?'

Paul patted the hard bulge on his hip.

'Did the Captain say you could take it?'

'Yes,' said Paul, but she knew that he was lying.

'What would I do, if someone went out the back gate?'

'Yell for me. Stop him somehow. Scare the horse. Throw stones. Anything. Go on, Dora. What's the matter?'

'They say the house is haunted.'

'So what? You don't believe that, do you?'

'I don't know.'

'Don't tell me you've let Uncle scare you. I thought you were supposed to be as tough as me.'

'I am.' Glancing fearfully about her, she ran up the uneven drive, wishing they had brought a dog. The drive was not long, and she kept her eyes fixed on the house, as if she expected it to move towards her, or all the windows to fly up and the dark front door to swing wide at her approach.

When she reached the house, she stopped and went more slowly, her throat thick with the beating of her heart, as if it were lodged under her chin. The statue of a Greek woman, draped, thick-legged, with bird lime in her piled hair, watched her with smooth stone eyeballs as she crossed the spread of grass-grown gravel under the terrace and went round the side of the house to look over the bridge.

The lake was an artificially swollen section of the stream which ran through the park. The narrow, humped bridge with knobless urns and beakless eagles on its parapet, crossed the water near the house.

Holding her breath, Dora crept up one side of the bridge, keeping low under the parapet. There was no one at the back gate beyond the outbuildings, and no tracks of anything on wheels or hooves.

Between the bridge and the house was a dark and dangerous hole where the stream ran underground beneath the terrace. The sluggish water was full of cans and beer bottles, and a mass of sodden newspaper clung to the grating. A cheerless spot to picnic, but it was private property, therefore desirable. A dead blackbird floated among the refuse, and something that might have been a rat. Above the water, a balcony curved out from a second floor window in the turret. Good place to get rid of unwanted guests.

163

No, she was not afraid. Lonely. If she called out to Paul, for the reassurance of his strong young voice, he might think it was her signal and leave his post. Alone. Too small and exposed in the flat white light. But when the moon sailed into a cloud and it was suddenly a night of depths and mysteries, she would not look at the dark mass of the house, but stood with her head back and her eyes fixed on the silver-trimmed cloud, waiting for it to be light again.

Ever since she had started up the drive. she had been struggling inside her head to push back the remembrance of the things she had heard about this house. The neighbourhood children knew that it was haunted. That was nothing, since they could conjure up a haunt in a harmless bungalow less than ten years old, if it was the only empty place in the village.

But it was Uncle's stories ... Uncle's tales of ice-cold babies and white weeping women and long ago tragedies that hung about the grey unforgetting house like mist wraiths round the trunks of elms.

Was it on this terrace that the old woman with the macaw on her shoulder had walked back and forth, back and forth, watching for the soldier son who never came back until the knocking of his spirit at the door summoned her to him?

Which door? She spun away from the wide front entrance to the little oak door set low and secret in the turret, to catch it at whatever tricks it – *what was that?* Which door? It was a house of doors, all sealed. A house of windows, all empty. Which bedroom casement had framed, so long ago, the violent quarrels and passionate embraces of the husband and wife who had looked out too late, too late to see their little wilting daughter walk unaware into the lake?

The tales were no more than embellished legends, or pure inventions by Uncle. And yet ... When the moon slipped into darkness, Dora stared and stared at the lake in case the child's white drowning arm should break the surface before the light came through again to show the mirror of the water intact.

And the headless horseman. She fought to keep him back, but – Oh, how could people picnic cheerfully here with the air so charged with dread? Galloping into the front of her mind came the gay young Lord of the Manor who had put his hunter at the steep-sided brook for a bet, and broken the horse's neck as well as his own.

His wife had been seen by several generations, wringing her sad white hands along the terrace walk. Some said that the statue was her turned to stone, watching at the corner of the parapet for the horse that galloped like thunder through the park with nothing on the end of its neck where the head should have been, and nothing on the end of the neck of the man who rode it.

Hollow on the turf of the hill drummed the galloping hooves. Caught in the moonlight between the turret wall and the bridge, hollow in the cave of her fear drummed Dora's heart. A handful of cloud trailed its shadow across her as she swung round, and in the moment when the moon rode clear, she saw the cold stone eyes of the statue move in a white glint of welcome.

Very near now, round the corner of the house, the hoofs spattered on the gravel, and Dora backed against the turret, closed her eyes and pressed her hands over them. Over the bridge in a thick tattoo of sound went the galloping hoofs, and were gone. Dora screamed: 'Paul! Paul!' and ran sobbing back down the driveway.

'Who was it? Couldn't you stop him? Where'd he go? Did you see him?'

Breathless, her sobs were dry. 'I couldn't look,' she gasped. 'I thought it was the headless horseman.'

She thought that he would rend her, but he said nothing. He looked at her queerly for a moment, and then was gone, pattering up the drive with the heels of his white shoes flying like rabbit scuts and disappearing in the long shadows flung downhill by the horse.

'The Captain wants to see you.' Paul looked over the door of the stable where Dora was brushing the mud off Spot.

She looked round and saw his face, and her own face fell. 'What have I done?'

'He's wild.' Paul kicked at the bottom of the door, and the circus pony moved his spotted head up and down in protest. 'He had a flat tyre coming back from town last night, and he'd forgotten to get his spare mended. He stopped a car and asked them to phone me to come for him in the truck.'

'That's done it.'

'No Paul. No truck. He and Mrs Sheppard had to walk three miles to get a car.'

With anyone else, Dora might have said: 'Do 'em good,' but the Captain and Anna Sheppard were both people she loved, and therefore privileged to resent it.

'What did he say?'

'Enough. I try to tell him it's not your fault, but he's in a shocking temper, and he raps out: "She was with you, wasn't she?" '

Dora had only once been in trouble with the Captain, over a stable door left unbolted, and she had not forgotten it. Feeling sick and shaky, she dropped the brush and curry comb into her grooming box and came out into the yard. She looked towards the house, then looked at Paul uncertaintly. 'Now?'

'Yup.'

'By myself?'

'Yup.'

'If we'd only caught someone –'

'Yup.' As she turned to drag her feet away, Paul said abruptly: 'They found the horse.'

'Where?'

'Not far from the Manor. I went the wrong way when I lost his tracks on the road. They found him this morning outside his own field. Got there somehow dot and carry with a pulled tendon. Dead lame now, of course.'

'It was my fault. Oh Paul – it was my fault!'

'No,' Paul said bitterly. 'It was mine. I should have had the sense to take a man with me.'

Dora began to cry. 'Save the tears,' he said brutally, 'till you hear whose horse it was.'

She did not want to know. It was a horse, and she had failed it.

'It was the blacksmith's old pony that his daughter rides. The one that was in the accident.'

Dora turned and ran from him towards the house. The Cap-

166

tain's anger was an insignificant thing now. Nothing that he said could make it any worse.

When the blacksmith's daughter had come out of the hospital in a wheelchair, and they knew that she would never walk again, she and her father, who were both straightforward, sensible people, had said to each other: That doesn't mean not ride again.

Afterwards, they could not remember which one of them had said it first. Riding had always been Moll's delight, and although there had never been any money, there had somehow always been some kind of scruffy pony or makeshift horse ever since she was six. The horse she had at the time of the accident, bought for ten pounds and an old bicycle, was a shy, tricky, tearaway thing, no use for their new plan, which they were not confiding to her mother.

The blacksmith exchanged it for a dead quiet pony called Pogo, who had taught dozens of children to ride, and had long ago replaced ambition with ambling kindliness. Nothing upset him. He had never been known to shy or balk or take charge, even with the feeblest novice. He was as foolproof as an armchair.

Moll made a face when she saw him, for he was plain and blunt, with thick hairy legs, and a mass of mane and forelock like a sheepdog. But he was perfect for their plan, and soon she forgot his looks, and even fancied him as a charger, for he had changed her futile criplehood to something approaching independence.

'For the love of heaven, what are they doing now?' Her mother had come running out of the forge cottage like a squawking hen when she realized that the pit her husband had been digging in the back garden was not for rubbish, and that the common old pony he had brought home was not for himself.

'Be quiet, Mum,' Molly called anxiously from her wheelchair, but her father had said: 'Come on, woman, come on. Make all the racket you want, and you'll see how safe he is.'

When his wife was out, and in the early morning before she was up, he had been training Pogo to back quietly down the gently sloping end of the long pit and stand in there like a rock until he was told. 'Get up.'

Although she screamed and would have run to clutch her daughter if her husband had not grabbed and held her, for she was a silly hysterical woman with none of the fortitude of the other two, the pony stood stock still, not even moving his head, while Moll edged her chair beside the hole, leaned over to grab his thick mane, and pulled her useless legs across the saddle.

For a year she rode him like this, ambling about the fields and green tracks, and even on the roads, for twelve racing cars flat out with blaring horns could have shaved by Pogo without him flicking an ear. After a while, even the mother calmed down, when she saw the safety and good sense of him, and the new life he had given to Moll.

She could go riding whenever she wanted, just as she used to when she could walk as well. Trundling her chair, she would lead the pony from the stable with her arm through the reins, and leave him in front of the pit while she manoeuvred herself along the edge behind him so that the wheels were between the concrete blocks which would stop the chair toppling when she climbed back into it.

Often before she said: 'Get back,' he would back himself down the slope as cautiously as an old man lowering himself into an armchair, turn his head for her sugar when he was in place, and then stand braced and still with the oddest look of responsibility in his eye until her strong arms had pulled her on to his back. When she said: 'Get up,' and never before, he would walk smoothly up the slope, look round him as if he had come up out of a mine, and plod off with her.

When they returned, she would back him down into the pit and slide herself into the wedged wheelchair, and Pogo would come up to ground level again and potter off to his stable to be unsaddled.

Apart from the saddle and bridle, Moll and Pogo were independent. Her father was working on a special girth she could tighten from her chair, and they were teaching Pogo to hold his head low to her for the bridle, when the Night Riders took him from his field and left him with a rasping wind, and a foreleg he could scarcely put to the ground.

Moll did not go out very much after that, except to the stable, and it was hard to make her take an interest in anything.

With the muscle tendon pulled away from the bone behind the knee, it would be months before Pogo could work again. 'I'll get you another pony, love,' the blacksmith said, but Moll said, with truth: 'We can't afford it, and keep Pogo too.'

Neither suggested that they might get rid of Pogo, and the mother, who was quite converted, said: 'You'd never find another like him anyway.'

Then Paul came and offered to lend them Cobbler's Dream. He came riding the half blind pony, so that they could see how quiet he was, and left him standing outside the forge with his reins down on the ground like a cow pony, so that they could see how dependable he was.

At first, Moll shook her head like a bull, and muttered un-graciously: 'No . . . no. It wouldn't do.'

'I doubt we could trust him, Paul,' the blacksmith said. 'No offence meant, but him being a show jumper and that. And the poor brute can't hardly see.'

'Not trust the Cobbler!' Paul was shocked. 'You could put a new born baby on him and he'd bring it safe home. He can see enough with half an eye. He'll never jump again, that's true, but he'll never stumble either, if you take him slow. You know him, Moll. You've seen him working in the cart. I could train him for this in a week. He'd love it, and you – you'll never know you've lived till you've ridden him.'

Moll laughed for the first time since Pogo was found by the gate with his head down and his foreleg dangling.

'You're daft,' she said. 'Cobb's well off where he is. You don't want to send him here.'

'Yes, I do. I must. Don't you see, Moll, what happened to your pony – it was my fault. We could have stopped him in time if we –'

'We? I thought you was alone.'

'I was. It was my fault. That's why I want you to have Cobby. I'll work with him here till he knows you, and then – well, just ride him over to the Farm whenever you can, there's a good girl.'

'And another thing.' They hadn't said yes and they hadn't

said no, but Paul had set his heart on this, so it was as good as done. 'Keep him in at night. If you hadn't left Pogo –'

'Don't let that animal eat my wallflowers!' The mother changed the subject with quick clumsiness, but Moll gripped the arms of her chair and said fiercely: 'And if I hadn't gone pillion with poor Ricky, I'd have my legs.'

'I'm sorry.' Paul looked away. 'I wasn't trying to be smart. I was just afraid that Cobby – but if you don't want him, forget it.'

He went to the door. The mother was clucking: '... so ashamed ... how could you ... never heard you speak so sharp.'

Ignoring her, Moll looked at her father. 'We can't afford to keep two ponies.'

'If I can get the Captain to have Pogo at the Farm, then will you take the Cobbler?'

'Yes,' said Moll. 'Yes. Thank you, Paul.'

Chapter Fourteen

There was a moment during that long walk on the Easter Saturday night when Paul and Dora had taken the truck, when Anna Sheppard was afraid of what the Captain was going to say.

Why afraid? Because she was not prepared.

He still talked to her about Roxanne, as if he had neither forgotten her, nor given up hope. So how could Anna answer if he spoke to her of love?

But he did not speak of it, and so there was nothing to answer. After he had kissed her while they were resting in the smooth armchair roots of a great beech tree, he looked at her for a moment gravely – that was the moment which threw her into alarm. Then he got up, pulled her to her feet, and walked on as if nothing had happened.

And what, after all, had happened? A kiss in the blue-white moonlight because she was tired and they were friends, and he thought it was the thing to do. But when she looked up at his face as they walked, she saw that he was angry. Surely not still because they had waited an hour at the crossroads and Paul had not come. She tried to talk to him, but he did not want to talk. Was he angry with Anna for liking him to kiss her, or for not liking it enough? With another man, she might have discussed it. With the Captain, it was very difficult to reopen a subject after he had closed it, especially when he was walking down the middle of the shining road so fast that it was all she could do to keep pace without letting him notice her effort.

As she trotted along with her feet in agony inside the pretty shoes that had not expected to walk home, she sought for some remark that would show him that she could be serious about the kiss if he liked, or she could take it or leave it if that was the way he felt.

Nothing came. There was no such remark to cover everything. Then they were at the garage, and throwing pebbles at the window to wake the man. The Captain prowled restlessly round the pumps while he was dressing, and when they were in the taxi, there was no chance to say anything except that she had not minded the walk and that she hoped he would not be angry with Paul in the morning.

'Was he angry with Paul?' she asked Dora when she came to the Farm the following week.

'Not half,' said Dora. 'And me too. And yet if he'd been at home, he'd have gone off after the pony the same as we did.'

. She showed Anna Pogo, contentedly established in the corner box. 'He's all right,' she grudged him, smacking his spoiled whiskered nose lightly, 'but no personality. Nothing like Cobby. Everybody misses that little horse, and Paul's like a mother who's lost her baby, even though it was his idea. I wish he hadn't done it. It makes me feel worse.'

'What about?'

'I panicked that night. Didn't Callie tell you? Paul told her the whole story when she was here with Mrs Berry.'

'Not that bit.'

'He's odd, like that. He told Moll's family that he went out after their pony alone. He'll lie about anything.'

'If it's to protect someone, I don't call it lies.'

'*He* does. He says he lies to protect himself. He wasn't going to let them know he gummed the whole thing up by taking a girl.'

'You said you weren't going to be angry with Paul,' Anna said to the Captain as soon as she saw him.

'Don't you start. I've had Tiny on my neck with her poor motherless boy refrain.' He looked at Anna half guiltily, half sulkily, like a child confessing. 'I yelled at Dora too.'

'She didn't tell me.'

'Why should she? There's too much of everybody telling everybody everything. Place is like a blasted confessional.'

'She probably would have if I had told her that you were angry with me first.' It was easier to bring it up now in daylight in the cramped, untidy office where she felt at home than it had been on the moonlit road between the black and white beeches, with the memory of his kiss too close.

'I wasn't angry with you, Anna. With myself. I shouldn't have kissed you. Should I?'

He looked down and scrabbled with his fingers on the desk, and before Anna could answer – but what could she answer? – he said in a rush: 'I had a letter from Roxanne last week. Someone told her where I was. I'm going to see her.' He got up and went round the desk to where Anna was standing uncertainly. 'She's coming here. Here. It's almost seven years. I–' He screwed up his face 'I shan't know what to say to her.'

'Is she married?'

'She was. Divorced a year ago. "Got away in time," was how she put it.'

'I'm very happy for you,' Anna said smoothly, to cover her agitation.

'You mean, you think she –' He looked a little stunned, as if he had not dared to hope for this.

'Of course.' It was quite easy to keep up the pretence of being casual and pleased, once you had made the painful start. 'You'll have to make your best impression.' She frowned at his torn pullover, his terrible old jacket with Tiny's leather binding curling off the cuffs. 'We'll have to smarten you up a bit. You can't have looked like that when she knew you in the Army. Shall I help you to choose a new suit? And you could go to Peter's barber. He's very good'

'Listen, Anna.' He looked distressed at the idea of being chiselled out of his rustic mould. 'I wish you wouldn't bother.'

'But I *want* to.'

Fool, she had been. Fool she was. Even while he kissed her under the tree and she had been pleased to let him, he had known that this girl was coming back to him. To cover her shame, she flung herself enthusiastically into the preparation of the Captain for his second chance with Roxanne.

The news leaked out through Callie, and Tiny's guesswork gave a fairly true assessment. Dora and Corinne, though jealous for an unreal second in which they forgot that they were seventeen and he was fifty-one, swung back immediately with suggestions for his clothes, and offers of cushions and lamps for the unlovely drawing-room. The Captain found himself, to his dismay, being garnished and groomed by the women like a Cretan athlete preparing to face the Minoan bull.

Tiny kept out of it. She was against the Captain marrying anyone, and certainly not the laughing girl whose picture she would turn down on its face when she was cleaning his room because she did not like the cocksure way it looked at her.

On the morning that Roxanne was to come, she prepared an excellent cold lunch and then strode in her beret and leather jacket to the stables and told the Captain that she was going out.

'You can't.'

'It's the last day of the sales.' Tiny pulled on baggy woollen gloves that were the same colour and style as a child's. 'Everything is laid out nice in the dining-room. I hope you have a very agreeable time,' she said gloomily, and marched off to the bus stop, swinging a canvas shopping bag round her ankles as if she were walking through a cloud of mosquitoes.

An hour later, Slugger Jones remarked to no one in particular: 'There's a strange woman, up at the house. I don't know how she got in,' he said, although the farmhouse doors were never locked, 'but she's talking about seeing the Captain.' He spoke with suspicion. The preparations for the coming of Roxanne had passed him by.

'It's her!' Corinne hissed at Dora.

'It's her, she says,' Slugger told the dull-eyed Lancelot, whose broad cob's head was hung over the nearest stable door. 'You might ask her who, and why doesn't she do something about it? People wandering about the house alone and all the silver out. It isn't right.'

Dora went to find the Captain, 'She's too early. You haven't got your new suit on. Mrs Sheppard will be terribly upset.'

'That's her funeral,' the Captain said uncharitably, and ran towards the house.

'Eager as a boy,' Corinne crooned with her yellow-tailed head on one side, although she for one would weep buckets at the Captain's wedding.

It was torture for them not to know what was going on in the house, but Paul was up in his room changing, and he heard a few remarks from the hall, and invented a few more, and since the Captain brought the dark, vivid girl out to see the

174

horses when Dora was sweeping the yard, and since Corinne was conveniently feeding Tiny's baby animals when he brought her back through the kitchen, they were able between them to piece together the whole drama of the return of Roxanne.

CAPTAIN (*panting gently, a little too boyish, from nerves*): Oh, hul*lo*! You're early. I shouldn't be in these old clothes.

ROXANNE: I don't mind, darling.

'*You made that up,*' the girls protested, but Paul swore to it, '*and of course,*' Dora commented when they were relaying the dialogue later to Anna, who scolded them at first for eavesdropping, and then listened shamelessly, '*she's the kind of woman who'd call the postman darling.*'

CAPTAIN: I was going to change.

ROXANNE: Don't worry about me. I heard you'd gone quite native. Teddy told me when he wrote that he'd been here. 'Everything subtly charged with his favourite perfume,' was how he put it.

CAPTAIN (*laughing it off*): Yours too, you used to say.

ROXANNE: Oh, I grew out of *that* long ago. I've grown in and out of six dozen crazes since you knew me. Wasn't I horsey though? You could have driven a bus through my legs. But horses are a phase, I think, like jazz, and bearded men.

'*Try again, Paul. They couldn't have been in the hall all that time.*'

'*They left the drawing-room door open. I was hanging over the stairs.*'

CAPTAIN: What would you like to drink? Is it still gimlets?

ROXANNE: The memory of the man. But I grew out of that too. Oh, all right, then, if you want to be sentimental. (*A pause. Bottles. Ice. The Captain dropping something.*) To us, darling. (*The clink of glasses.*)

'*At least, I thought I heard that,*' Paul amended. '*They'd shut the door by then. I came downstairs and stuck my eye in the keyhole, but I couldn't see much. Just the Captain lighting his pipe –*'

'*That Pipe! That vile-smelling thing – and before lunch. Oh, he ought to be shot.*'

'*Some romance,*' Corinne said dolefully. '*What can you do with him?*'

There were a few more remarks that Paul claimed to have heard, or thought he might have heard, and then he had to go across the road, because Mrs Catchpole was giving him lunch with the girls.

Dora did not have to sweep the stable yard after lunch, since it had been swept this morning and she was off duty anyway, but she guessed that the Captain would never let anyone get away without seeing the horses, so she sneaked back across the road without telling the others, and got the broom.

CAPTAIN (*unseen on the cinder path behind the bushes*): Only some of them are in the stables. The others are out in the fields. We can go and see them if your shoes are all right. It's a bit muddy.

ROXANNE: It always is. Let's not bother. (*They come into the yard and he begins to take her on the full tour, but she moves quickly ahead from box to box, so that he can't embark on a long story about each horse.*) What a ghastly looking animal. (*At Spot's stable.*) Where on earth did you get it?

CAPTAIN (*a little stiffly*): From a circus. He's part Appaloosa. Look – put your finger on him. You can feel the spots.

ROXANNE (*pouting derisively at Spot, as if he were her own face in the mirror*): He looks like a table.

CAPTAIN: So would you if people had been jumping up and down on your back for fifteen years. He's very old.

ROXANNE: Too old, poor thing. Look, his eye is all runny. Why do you keep him alive?

CAPTAIN (*patiently*): I told you, that's the whole point of the Farm. We don't believe in killing any animal that can still enjoy the kind of life we can give.

ROXANNE (*lightly, moving on*): Some people would say it was a waste of money.

'I like it,' said Corinne, sucking her lips. 'It's good, but the only snag is they must have been yelling, for you to have heard all that.'

'I was getting closer with the broom. Sweeping quietly, you know, like part of the yard, hoping they wouldn't notice me.'

CAPTAIN: Dora – I thought you were off.

DORA: The yard was a mess. And it's such a nice day, I thought we might get visitors this afternoon.

'Captain's pet.'

'I had to have an excuse for being there, didn't I?'

CAPTAIN: And we have a visitor already. Rox, this is Dora, my best stable worker.

'It's a lie,' Paul said.

'All right. One of my best stable workers.'

ROXANNE (*Affable. She is very pretty, though a little hard, with a wide crimson smile and fabulous make-up*): How do you do, dear.

DORA (*wipes hand on trousers and gives it to Roxanne, feeling like a crossing sweeper.*)

ROXANNE (*Moving on round the boxes*): She's very young. And all the horses are so old. What a funny place this is.

CAPTAIN (*Moving with her, still eager for the guided tour*): This is Nigger. Don't touch his head. He's been very brutally treated. Here's Dolly, the one I was telling you about, who gave me this. (*Hand to scar.*)

'He never talks about it.'

'She must have made him tell her.'

ROXANNE: And you kept her?

CAPTAIN: Why not? It wasn't her fault. She's lovely now. I can do anything with her. And here's our mule, Willy. He's in today because he's coughing. And this is Mrs Berry, poor old soul. Well, she's a gelding really, but we –

ROXANNE: They're your life, aren't they? (*Wonderingly, half to herself.*) They're your whole life.

CAPTAIN (*Inside Fanny's stable, checking the lump inside her cheek*): Who? Oh – (*His head comes over the door*) You mean the horses. Well, look – they'd have to be in a place like this.

'Hell of a long sweep you were having,' Paul said. 'What were you using – a toothbrush?'

'I'm hidden in the donkey's box by now, mucking out, if anyone wants to look in.'

ROXANNE: You haven't changed at all. Horses always came first.

CAPTAIN: So they did with you.

ROXANNE (*Impatiently*): Oh, when I was a kid. But there are too many other things. Horsey people are too one-track, like doggy women. I wish you could see the house I have now. It's in a mews. Stiff with actors and ballet dancers. Quite perfect. And a fantastic Frenchman next door who designed my whole colour scheme. (*She smiles.*) No saddles –

'*I thought you were mucking out the donkeys.*'

'*You don't have to see a person smile. You can hear it in their voice.*'

– on the back of the sofa now.

CAPTAIN: Remember the bridle on the doorknob – how it used to annoy your father?

ROXANNE: You've got a better memory than me.

'*When I came out of the donkeys, they were leaning over the door, one on each side, cosy, with their elbows touching.*'

'*Go on. Then he kissed her,*' Paul said. '*Right there with you looking on. Don't ever call me a liar again.*'

'*Well, he didn't, so nyah.*'

'*Quite right. He's much too old for her.*'

'*How do you know? You didn't see her.*'

'*I didn't need to, with you two on the job.*'

'*I give her about twenty-eight,*' Corinne said, '*and that's being charitable. But she could be his daughter, and when they came into the kitchen, they were laughing and kidding, as if she was.*'

CAPTAIN (*Rather sharply, since he thought everyone was out*): What are you doing?

CORINNE: Feeding the babies.

ROXANNE: This place is like a nursery. Even the horses are in their second childhood. (*She looks round the kitchen, at Tiny's effervescent pickle crock, the bird cages with open doors, the cat playing inside an agitated brown paper bag, the dogs and puppies, the wired-in box for the baby squirrel, the halter ropes on the door hook, the muddy boots, the goldfish, the guppies, and she laughs.*) You're in your element here. (*A pause.*) Happy?

CAPTAIN (*He has his head in the hall cupboard, getting out her coat. His reply is inaudible.*)

ROXANNE (*With a sort of affectionate sadness, as if she*

were handing him over to another woman): I'm very glad for you.

'She went away then,' Corinne said. 'I ran upstairs and looked out of the window. She had a gorgeous coat and a terrific car. It made that rich snarling noise when she zoomed off.'

They had all seen it. Paul said: 'How on earth does an old geezer like him get a girl like that?'

'He hasn't got her,' Dora said. 'If you want to know what I think – I don't think she'll come back.'

'How sad,' Anna said when they told her. 'Oh, how sad for him after he's waited all these years.'

'That's what we thought,' Dora said. 'But hear this. You know how dodgy he was before she came? He's as jolly as a porpoise now. Hung a plastic bag over his new suit, Tiny says, like a shroud, and been whistling the same bit of tune ever since.'

Chapter Fifteen

'If the Cobbler wasn't doing such a good job for Moll,' Paul said, 'I'd have him back. I miss that little horse like nobody's business.'

'I wonder what he thinks,' Dora said. 'You don't suppose he thinks you've sold him?'

'He trusts me more than that. He thinks it's just a job.'

'Does a horse think, anyway? When they're standing there resting a back foot, with their eyes half closed, is it all just a blank, or are their brains working?'

'The Cobbler's is,' Paul said quickly. 'He thinks about the next meal, and all those yards and yards of gut start to gurgle. And he thinks about what it's like to be a horse. He feels himself, standing inside his four legs and his arched neck and his strong red body, with his beautiful long tail swinging – swat, swat –'

'How do you know?'

'If I stand and watch him long enough, I know what it's like to be him,' Paul said.

Dora did not laugh. He had not thought she would, or he would not have told her. She said: 'That's why you'll always stay with him.'

'If I can. But if the Captain ever found out what I'd done and where I'd been, he wouldn't keep me.'

'You should have told him,' said Dora, who could never have lived contentedly with a secret like that.

'He'd never trust me again.'

'Oh, he would.'

Paul shook his head. 'I don't know. Maybe I should be moving on anyway. Go out and get me a job that's got some future in it.'

'Why? You like the Farm. You told me you'd never been happy before you came.'

'Well, suppose I get married – have kids one day? Not much of a future, mouldering away in some little cottage like Uncle –'

'Uncle isn't mouldering. He's had the life he wanted. What's the good of going out and earning hundreds of pounds if you have to be shut up in some dreary office? Well – you'd never get that kind of job anyway. You're too ignorant. But a dreary factory then. And what would you do with that chestnut pony you know what it feels like to be?'

'Ah,' said Paul. 'That's it.'

One day when Dora was in town, she ran into Ron Stryker among the Saturday market stalls. Dora was looking for some flowered cotton for Mrs Catchpole to make curtains. Ron, in a sharp new suit with a long tight jacket and infinitesimal coloured lapels, was at a junk stall, idly picking over tarnished buttons, blunt rusted weapons and old gramophone records.

They were glad to see each other. Dora had never disliked Ronnie as much as the others, because he made her laugh. Ron had no use for Dora as a girl – his kind of chick wore tights and very short skirts and had hair piled in fantastic shapes – but she was good for a joke and a scrap, like a boy, and being rather crooked himself, he respected her for being dead straight, which the chicks were not.

'So what's new?' he asked her. He had become slightly more American since he left the Farm. His bushy hair was punched down and stuck with grease, and sidewhiskers lay self-consciously on his tallow cheeks.

She told him some of the small details which loomed large in her days, like one of the donkeys being put down, and the new horse with the terrible collar galls, whose owner had gone to prison, and Ron fiddled vacantly with an ancient knife, slapping its decorated blade first on one palm, then on the other.

'How's his Lordship then?'

'The Captain? Oh, he's fine, he –'

'Nah.' Ron spat. He had not spat when he was at the Farm,

but he was working down at the warehouses now. 'You know who I mean. Your friend Paul.'

'He's fine. He'll *love* to know you asked after him,' Dora said, grinning.

' 'E might love to know too that I haven't forgot. I'll carry it to my dying day, what he done to me.'

'Paul never did you any harm.'

Ronnie snorted. 'So telling everybody it was me set light to the barn, that wasn't doing no harm, eh?'

'But he didn't!'

'Somebody did, and lost me me job. Not to mention references.'

'Nobody had to. Everyone knew you used to smoke in there.'

'The Captain didn't know.' His voice was quick and spiteful.

'He guessed. I don't smoke, and he knew Paul never did round the stables.'

'Little angel Curly,' Ron jeered. 'Don't kid yourself, girl. It was him split on me all right.'

'Why should he?'

'Oh – things. Get his own back. Old score. He knows where I find my friends,' Ron said darkly. 'How's the Cobbler then?' He abruptly changed the subject. 'Still running the place all his own way?'

Dora told him the story of Pogo, to which he listened with his head on one side, with interest, and how Paul had taken Cobby over to work for Moll, to make it up to her.

'Is that a fact?' Ron said, jabbing the blunted point of the knife against the edge of the stall. 'Is that a fact?'

'You either give me two guineas for that knife,' the junk dealer said, coming round from the other side of the stall, 'or put it down and clear off.'

'Wouldn't soil me 'ands with it.' Ron moved away from Dora into the crowd without saying good-bye.

It was a week later, and the moon was approaching the full again. There had been no trouble from the Night Riders since they had galloped poor Pogo into the ground, but Dora was restless, uneasy.

'Why does it always have to be a full moon on a Saturday?' she asked after supper.

'What will be, will be,' was Mrs Catchpole's unsatisfactory answer, and Uncle said: 'Sit down to something, and stop pacing like a caged jackal. We've got 'em licked now, for there's not a horse in these parts left loose at nights.'

'There's the gipsy ponies out on Easter Common.'

'Them young buzzards from town ain't going to tangle with no gipsies,' Uncle said. 'They may be fools, but they ain't heroes.'

Dora was looking out of her window across the road towards the stables, roofed with the snow of moonlight, when she saw an old car stop by the closed gate. The blacksmith got out, went through the gate, and turned off at the path through the shrubbery to go to the house.

Dora fell downstairs, flung a word to Mrs Catchpole, hooking a rug in the front room, and dashed across the road, pulling on a high-necked sweater as she ran, one shoe tied and the other flicking its laces round her foot.

'Moll? Is something wrong with Moll?' Running through the kitchen and into the hall, she met the broad back of the blacksmith, the Captain in the drawing-room doorway with his hand on the knob as if he had just come out, Paul on the stair-case in a running attitude, with both hands on the banister.

'It's Cobby.' Paul leaned over the banister and she saw his face, and the blacksmith turned, with a flat look of fear in his eyes and told her, in the dull voice of repetition: 'It was my club night. Moll's kept in with a cold, and the wife was to see the pony padlocked in after his feed. I come home a half hour ago and went to check him.'

'He's gone, Dora,' the Captain said, and the restless, indefinite worry that had hovered just out of sight all evening slid into focus as she remembered Ron Stryker's casual: 'How's the Cobbler then?' by the market stall.

The Night Riders. And she the traitor. The informer. 'Oh, Paul, I –' She and Paul were in the little truck, bucketing along the road behind the blacksmith and the Captain, his car going faster than he had ever dared to drive it. 'You know I met Ron? He knew where Cobby was. I told him.'

Paul nodded, his mouth a set line, his strong brown hands tense on the wheel.

Dora said nothing. Her stupidity was too gross for apology. Her fear was frozen too deep to voice. It had been her fault about Pogo. If anything happened to Cobbler's Dream, it would be her fault too.

At the fork in the road, the Captain zoomed ahead to follow the way that led round the back of the Manor and its park, and Paul turned right to follow the front road.

They passed the parking field for the racecourse and the cockeyed ticket booth, newly painted yellow for the point-to-point meeting next week. Paul had not spoken since they left the Farm. Now as they approached the Manor, he turned to Dora and smiled 'Don't be afraid.'

'I'm not afraid.' She leaned forward, staring grimly ahead as if she could force into her eyes a vision of the chestnut pony wandering harmlessly down the road. 'I won't let you down again.'

Paul said surprisingly: 'I liked it that you were afraid.'

'I thought you were angry.'

'About the horse. But you were just being a girl. I liked that better than when you try to be a boy.'

When they came in sight of the spiked iron fence of the park, Paul shut off the engine and coasted. They could be racing in the park. They had got away with it before. He put on the brakes and sat for a moment staring at nothing through the straight windscreen.

'If they do any harm to the Cobbler,' he said in a choked voice, 'I'll kill them.'

'I wish you hadn't brought the gun.'

'I don't.'

'Would you kill someone – for a horse?'

'For the Cobbler,' Paul corrected. 'I don't know. They just better not try me, that's all.'

He got out of the truck and ran to the gateway. There were the fresh tracks of a horse, but no tyre marks. The Cobbler's feet, the round, compact pony prints. He would know them anywhere.

The Captain was to leave the blacksmith at the back drive of the park before going on to search the fields on the other side of the village. Paul went back to the truck and drove it forward across the gateway, so that a horse could not get out. Keeping one on each side of the white gravelled drive so that they would be hidden somewhat by the long grass and scattered trees, he and Dora ran up the hill under the blind watching windows of the house.

The Greek woman stared at them with her sightless eyes, smooth as washed pebbles on the shore. Was Dora still afraid of her? Paul took her small calloused hand and pulled her up through the broken pillars on to the ruined terrace.

At their feet, grass and weed plants grew through the wide cracks between the tilting millstones. The crumbling parapet was rough with lichen under their hands as they stared down into the broad park, straining their ears to hear beyond the pounding of their hearts.

'Better go back down,' Paul said. 'There's nothing –'

A shout, a wild scream, and a yell of hysterical laughter, and over the hollow bridge, his tail streaming like water, his mouth and shoulders dropping foam, came Cobby, with the long-haired, long-legged boy flailing him like a demon.

Paul raised the revolver and fired, the boy laughed like a ghoul and galloped on wildly down over the rough turf between the trees. Paul jumped on to the parapet, dropped down and started to run, leaving Dora to scramble after him.

'Spread out!' The blacksmith was over the bridge and coming up behind them, and as they neared the bottom of the hill, they saw Cobby swerve away from the truck at the gate and try to stop. He slid in the mud and was down on his knee, righted himself, and wheeled back as the boy jerked his head round savagely, and for an instant Paul and the Hyena stared at each other, with the blind, blown pony's head flung up between them.

Paul knew that he could not trust himself to fire without hitting the pony, but the Hyena did not know it. His shifty black eyes were trapped and wild under the lank flop of hair. He saw the gun and the murder in Paul's eyes, the memory stored up, and the moment's desperation. He saw Dora, off to the side, raise her arm to fling a stone. He saw the burly man on the other side of the drive running towards him holding a stake like a club.

Again the blood-curdling laugh, half terror, half bravado, as he wrenched the pony round and drove him like a madman towards the park fence where the twisted iron spikes glinted in the moon's light above the dragging undergrowth.

It was an impossible jump. With this lunatic on its back, galloping flat out downhill on the rough ground, a sighted horse would not have a chance. For a pony with one eye gone and the other half gone ... Seeing already what the spikes would do when he rose at the terrible fence and failed, Paul prayed that he would stop, balk, swerve away from the vicious barrier that stood between the Hyena and escape.

But the Cobbler had never stopped or swerved when he was ridden strong. How much could he see? He could see and sense that there was an obstacle before him. He was being beaten on, and he had never failed to rise to the challenge of a big jump. But this –

This is it, Cobb. This is it for you and me both. I'm with you boy, I – With a tremendous effort, Paul surged his spirit forward until he was suddenly one with the Cobbler, riding him, possessing him, being him – Now!

He felt the gathering of muscle, the desperate thrust of the quarters, the lift and surge as the wicked spikes sailed past below, and then the jar and lurch as he landed and pitched forward, nose blindly down. He half recovered, and stumbled again on the edge of the grass, throwing the boy sprawling like a long-legged dummy on to the road to lie with his bloodied face upturned to the benevolent moonlight.

'Is he dead?' Paul was over the fence somehow, tearing his clothes, but Dora was stuck on the other side.

'Knocked out.' He straightened up and went to where the chestnut pony was standing unconcerned a few yards off, tearing at the roadside grass like a starving castaway.

'But why?' Dora asked, when the blacksmith had gone off in the truck carrying the inert Hyena, with instructions to dump him at the corner of one particular warehouse by the river –

Paul was very exact about the spot – and hurry away unseen. 'Why not the Police?'

'No need. He won't ride again.'

'But he turned you in.'

'So what?' They were walking along the road for home with the Cobbler, one on each side, the pony's sage nodding head between them. 'If I got him gaoled now, it wouldn't undo my time in Borstal.'

'You didn't tell in court,' Dora said, 'and you told me it was because you were afraid of what that lot would do to you. You didn't tell on that horrible fat child, and you told me it was because you needed her for blackmail. I'm disappointed in you, Paul. You lie all the time, and boast how mean you are, but who have you ever hurt with your lies? I've got a terrible feeling that you're not as tough as you think.'

'I didn't turn the Hyena in this time,' Paul lied indefatigably, 'because I didn't want to get you involved.'

They were half-way home when the Captain's car overtook them. Paul found himself suddenly tongue-tied, unable to tell the details of what had happened; but Dora was a stream in flood, practising on the Captain the story of the Great Leap of Cobbler's Dream, which she would tell so many times hereafter.

'You'll never believe it,' she said. 'You will simply and absolutely never believe it. We'll take you back tomorrow and show you where – oh, but you'll never believe it.'

'Am I so cynical?'

Dora looked at Paul. 'Would anyone believe it?'

'Quite a leap, wasn't it?' Paul grinned and slapped the pony's hot wet neck. 'Trust the Cobbler.'

'Is this the boy who helped to put you in Borstal?' the Captain asked abruptly, when Paul and Dora had told him as much as they thought he should know.

Paul looked at Dora. They both looked at Tiny, who had wandered in with her hands under the bosom of her apron to hear the story. Her large face, with its hint of moustache, gave away less than an Indian squaw. They looked back at the Captain, one eyebrow raised, waiting with a half smile.

Paul licked his lips and said nervously: 'I didn't think you knew.'

'I've known all along. Last year, when I telephoned that nasty child's father to make sure you hadn't stolen Cobby, he told me.'

'Ah yes.' Paul let his breath out in a long sigh. 'He would, of course.'

'And that degenerate in the cowboy boots, he came snooping up to hint at your shocking past when you'd only been here a week. When I wouldn't listen, he told it to Tiny.'

'All this time – why didn't you tell me you knew?'

'I wanted you to tell me yourself, Paul. It's never made any difference to the way I feel about you. I was waiting for you to trust me enough to tell me.'

'All right,' Paul said. 'I do. And while we're at it, I'll tell you something else. You won't like this, Dora, because I lied to you to try and make you think better of me. I didn't want anyone to know what my mother was like. She – she denied me, like Peter did Christ, and I was ashamed. She isn't dead, like I told you all she was. She's alive –' his voice was rising feverishly – 'she's alive and I hate her. She didn't want me. She never wanted me. When she turned against me in court, I killed her in my mind. It wasn't all a lie when I told you she was dead. She's dead for me, d'you hear! Dead –' He turned and flung up his arm against the wall like a child, and buried his face in it.

'Oh that,' said Tiny comfortably, pushing out the front of her apron with her folded hands. 'Don't bother about that little detail. I've known it for ages.'

Dora and the Captain stared at her, and Paul whipped round and stood with his hands flat against the wall behind him.

'I didn't tell anybody, because I didn't think it was anyone's business, even yours, since you were getting along so nicely without her. I flatter myself I'm a much better mother to you than ever she was, and so I told her.'

'*You've seen her!*'

'Certainly I've seen her. She came here one day when everyone but me and Jones was out – oh, back about last July, I think it was, because that big white dog was a puppy then, and fell over trying to jump up and bite her. She wanted you back, but

188

with what I knew and what I guessed, I didn't think she ought to have you.'

'Tiny,' the Captain said, a little shocked, 'you can't do that, I don't think, with someone's own child.'

'Who can't? He was over eighteen. And she didn't really want him anyway. Some man had let her down, I guessed, and she thought her son could support her till she found another. I told her to go and boil her head, as I'd tell her again if she was to come back bothering us – *which* I doubt she'll dare.'

She brought her hands out from under her apron and stood belligerent, massive bare arms folded, chin stuck out pugnaciously.

'Er – Tiny,' the Captain cleared his throat, 'how did you get rid of her?'

Tiny gave a growl of a laugh. 'I'm not an ex-wrestler for nothing, you know, and my Jones can still weigh-in with a useful punch if you point him in the right direction and set his arms going.'

Chapter Sixteen

They had built up the black brushwood jump again in the blossoming hedge at the top of the hill. They had set the two hurdles and the marker flag at the corner where the horses would bunch together to turn down into the plough. They had put up the ropes and the tents and the picketed enclosures, and as she went down the lane between the stable yard and the pastures, Callie's young eyes could see round the side of the hill the crop of glittering cars and the crowds and the bookies' gay umbrellas and the judges' wagonette outside the ropes with three men in bowler hats, and a huge woman standing up and waving like the Statue of Liberty.

'Hurry!' Callie looked back to call her mother and the Captain, treading at a walk the ground where she had run. 'I can see horses in the paddock. We'll miss the next race.'

They went through the first field, Callie zig-zagging from horse to grazing horse, and into the bottom field, where they sat on the fence together like birds and listened for the pounding hoofs beyond the brushwood which would herald the wave crest of leaping horses breaking over the top of the hill.

They watched two races, and saw five horses fall, and one woman, with the language of a docker, pick herself out of the mud and curse a broken collarbone.

When they came back to the stables, Callie was running ahead, screaming at Paul and Dora and Uncle, who were starting the evening work in the yard.

'I'm going to live here! I'm going to be here every day! Every day! Jean will be furious. I'm going to –'

Paul caught her and swung her round and buried a kiss in her slender throbbing neck.

'You landed that job at last then?' Uncle grumbled.

190

'Silly. Didn't you know? My mother's going to marry the Captain.'

It was a fine light evening and several racegoers stopped on their way home to visit the old horses. Many of the local people knew the Farm well, and liked to look in from time to time to savour the unusual peace of an enterprise that was unproductive of anything except content, and unprogressive in anything except the humanities. Strangers who had not been on this road before would see the sign curved over the gateway and speculate, or exclaim sentimentally, and often they would come curiously in under the arch, telling each other that it was touching, or fantastic, or could not happen in any other country in the world.

The yard was full of visitors. They pressed round the boxes, watching the horses being fed, and Uncle pushed his elbows through them muttering, but Paul and Dora showed off a little, as they always did when there was an admiring crowd, sensing themselves a spectacle along with the horses.

There was only one empty loose box, for Cobby was back, and the Captain had offered to keep Pogo, so that the blacksmith could get another pony while the leg mended.

That was how the Captain liked it. Full house, except for one or two empty boxes for emergencies. If Mrs Berry would keep away from the Irish ports for a while, and if Paul had abandoned his vague ideas about moving on and would stay here with the Cobbler, they were well set for the summer.

The Captain was talking to a nice woman with two clean children, telling them about the brown mare Pussycat who never did get to see the Queen, when Dora came threading through the crowd to him in an old pair of blue jeans, cut off in tatters at the bottom.

'It's all you need,' she said, her mouth serious, but her eyes flicking laughter. 'Mrs Berry is out there in the road with a milk horse in a cattle trailer, and ten women in two cars behind.'

The Captain smiled at the mother and children and drew Dora aside.

'Ten women?'

'From her road. The dairy's going mechanized and sending

191

their horses to the sales, so Mrs B. organized all these women to say that if the dairy wouldn't sell them the horse that brought them their milk for years, they wouldn't buy any more milk.'

'I see.' The Captain turned to see Mrs Berry in emerald green, with a long pheasant's feather in her hat, come bustling through the archway like Robin Hood, with her band of women behind her.

'I've brought you Peregrine!'

The people wandering in the middle of the yard made a space as she ran, all girlish and excited, to the Captain, her eyes flaming like brandied plums with the joy of rescue, her wet cherry mouth trembling with the realization of her planned surprise.

'Dora – naughty girl – said he looked fit enough to go to a home where he could work, but he's older than she is, and I don't like the look of his legs, poor darling, and he's pulled the same milk cart for fourteen years, and – oh, Captain, if you haven't got a stable free, we'll *build* one, the girls and I. Come out and see him. He has the face of a great philosopher. You'll not resist.'

She turned, and like a flock of birds, the other women went with her, except one, who looked like many children's grandmother, always good for a hug and a sixpence. She put her hand on the Captain's sleeve and said: 'Please take him. They told me your heart was soft for any horse.'

'I'm not sentimental, if that's what you –'

'Oh, nor am I. But old Ginger – that's his name really – he's worked so hard all his life, and earned his rest. You do take horses like that, don't you?'

The Captain smiled down at her. He was not tall, but she was a very small grandmother, in a brave hat, with honest blue eyes in a face that showed the lines of worry and sorrow and years of hard work for which there was no reward of green pastures this side of heaven.

'Of course,' he said. 'That's what we're here for.'